THE VENGEANCE WAY

"What's up, Lon?" Mark asked, seeing the strained expression on the Kid's face.

"When I told you I didn't know Sidewinder," the Kid replied in hardly more than a whisper, "I was wrong. I know him real good."

"Who is he?" asked Dusty. "And who's the Death Bringer?"

"She's a Mexican prisoner who was adopted into the Pehnane. They called her Fire Dancer, and she had a son. He got the name No Father on account of my pappy killing his old man the day I was born."

"So you know Sidewinder then," Hollenheimer said.

"I know him all right," agreed the Kid. "It was my knife that crippled him and the next time we meet, one of us is going to die."

QUANTITY SALES

Most Dell books are available at special quantity discounts when purchased in bulk by corporations, organizations, and special-interest groups. Custom imprinting or excerpting can also be done to fit special needs. For details write: Dell Publishing, 666 Fifth Avenue, New York, NY 10103. Attn.: Special Sales Department.

INDIVIDUAL SALES

Are there any Dell books you want but cannot find in your local stores? If so, you can order them directly from us. You can get any Dell book in print. Simply include the book's title, author, and ISBN number if you have it, along with a check or money order (no cash can be accepted) for the full retail price plus $2.00 to cover shipping and handling. Mail to: Dell Readers Service, P.O. Box 5057, Des Plaines, IL 60017.

SIDEWINDER

J.T. EDSON

A DELL BOOK

Published by
Dell Publishing
a division of
Bantam Doubleday Dell Publishing Group, Inc.
666 Fifth Avenue
New York, New York 10103

ISBN: 0-440-20293-0

Printed in the United States of America

Special Dell Edition

August 1990

Reprinted by arrangement with the author

10 9 8 7 6 5 4 3 2 1

RAD

THE FLOATING OUTFIT

J. T. Edson's famous stories of the range-tough Rebels who ran the OD Connected ranch—the legendary Floating Outfit—are related by plot and character; and yet each is an exciting, action-packed novel in itself. Read together or separately, they make up a magnificent and stunningly realistic saga of life on the frontier.

Western Adventure by
J. T. EDSON

For the fastest, most accurate combat pistol shot I ever knew, "Davo" Davidson of Ol Kalou, Kenya

CHAPTER ONE

A LESSON IN MATTERS COMANCHE

When delivering a lecture on the subject of "The Habits, Customs, and Lives of the Aboriginal Tribes of North America," Professor Otis J. Hollenheimer could pack to capacity a large hall in any major city of the United States or Europe. In the early 1870s he stood at the peak of the American scientific field and could claim to be an authority on his subject. Yet he sat silent and enthralled in the gun-decorated study of the big OD Connected ranch house, listening to a speaker who could barely read or write and whose formal classroom education had been nonexistent.

"Grandpappy Long Walker gave up the lance after he'd made his name," said the Ysabel Kid, continuing his lecture on the habits, customs, and lives of one of the aboriginal tribes of North America. "It got to be too much of a responsibility—like I said, a man who carried a lance had to be first in a fight and last out of it and could only come out a winner, or dead. But afore he gave it up, Grandpappy carried that lance and three times rode *pukutsi.*"

"*Pukutsi,*" repeated Hollenheimer. "That's the same as the Cheyennes' Contrary One, or the Crow's Crazy-Dog-Wishing-to-Die, isn't it? A warrior who did everything wrong and went unarmed into battle, fastened himself to the ground with an arrow through the sash he wore and stayed there singing until killed or his companions won the fight."

Admiration flickered on the Kid's Indian-dark, handsome, almost babyishly innocent-looking face. Few white men he had met, and certainly no fancy eastern schoolteaching dude, knew that much about Indians. However the professor had made a slight mistake.

"That's what *pukutsi* means among most Nemenuh bands," agreed the Kid, using the Comanches' name "The People." "Only the Pehnane, the Quick Stingers, Raiders you'd call them, got separated from the rest way back and made up a whole heap of new ideas. To us *pukutsi* meant something real different. When a man went *pukutsi* he used to strip to his breechclout and weapon belt. He wouldn't use his ordinary paint or medicine. All he did was make the sign of a red hand on his chest and his warhoss's right shoulder. Then he'd yell '*Pukutsi*,' jump on his hoss, and attack, no matter what odds he faced. Like a lance carrier he could only win or die."

"Then there was no difference?"

"A man going *pukutsi* could tote any weapons he wanted and went whether anybody followed him or not."

"Did you ever ride *pukutsi?*" Hollenheimer asked.

"I was a mite young for that," the Kid replied, sounding just a touch wistful. "I'd be rising fifteen when pappy took me off to fight the Yankees. Mind you, though, me and every other Pehnane boy wanted to carry the lance and ride *pukutsi* when we grew old enough."

"When you say Nemenuh," Hollenheimer said, "you mean the Comanche?"

"Sure."

"I thought they were called the Tshaoh?"

"That's what the other tribes called us, the Enemy People. Reckon that's just what we were to most of them. But every Comanche, no matter what band he belonged to, said Nemenuh. It means the People."

Standing before the fireplace in the well-lit study, the Ysabel Kid looked every inch a typical Texas cowhand. Six feet in height, lean as a steer fed in the greasewood country, with curly raven-black hair fresh barbered and neat; nothing gave a hint of how one so young in appearance had come to know so much about the West's toughest horse-Indian tribe. He wore a black bandana, shirt, and Levi's, with Comanche moccasins replacing his usual black boots while around the house. When outside he sported a low-crowned, Texas-style black Stetson hat and black leather gun-belt that carried an old walnut-handled Colt Dragoon revolver butt forward at the right side, and a sheathed James Black bowie knife at the left.

Apart from the somber hue of his clothes and the fact that one so young generally went in for the more modern, lighter Colt 1860 Army revolver instead of the thumb-busting 1847 Model Dragoon—and one of the first models produced to boot—little set the Kid apart from hundreds of other range-bred, cow-chasing Texans. Maybe his red-hazel eyes, reckless and old in wisdom, gave a hint at the true nature beneath the innocent face; but even they did not tell the full story.

The Kid had been born in the main village of the Pehnane Comanche band. Until his twelfth birthday the only white folk he knew had been men like his father, trappers, wild-horse hunters, traders. He grew up in the manner of a Pehnane boy and learned those things a brave-heart warrior must know.* While he never used the acquired skills—how to live off the Texas range country by hunting or upon roots, leaves, tree bark if necessary; to ride any horse ever foaled; handle weapons; move in silence no matter how thick the undergrowth; read sign and follow tracks; to raid, a polite name for stealing horses—among the Pehnane, all came in useful when joining the white men.

* Told in *Comanche*.

His mother had been daughter of Long Walker, the Pehnane's top war chief, and the French Creole *pairaivo,* chief wife, but had died shortly after his birth. His father was Sam Ysabel, a man of Kentuckian–black-Irish birth, whose courage and skill as a warrior endeared him to the Pehnane and bought him membership to the tribe. In the Kid's growing years Ysabel spent much time away from the village, trading and meat-hunting for the white settlements. Although the Pehnane name meant Wasps, Quick-Stingers, or Raiders, as the Kid said, the band lived at peace with their white neighbors; like all successful pacifists, the Pehnane made sure they possessed the necessary means to ensure their wishes be respected, and no Texan wanted fuss with such expert warriors. So the Kid and Ysabel never had to choose between one or other of their nations.

When the Civil War began, Ysabel accepted the offer to join John Singleton Mosby's Confederate cavalry regiment, and took Loncey with him. Their talents were much appreciated by Mosby's Raiders, but they received orders to return to Texas and organize the delivery of arms and other supplies from Mexico. This amounted to smuggling, at which the Ysabel family already accounted themselves expert, and they built up an effective organization that caused the Yankees much trouble.

After the war the Ysabels continued their smuggling, but on their own behalf. Then Sam Ysabel was murdered, and while seeking the men who killed his father, the Kid met up with somebody who changed the course of his life.* From being a smuggler, with one foot on the slippery slope that led to real lawbreaking, the Kid became a member of the OD Connected ranch crew and rode as part of the elite of the spread, Ole Devil's floating outfit. His many talents found legal use of much service to the community instead of being frittered away upon enter-

* Told in *The Ysabel Kid.*

4

prises that would eventually bring him into serious conflict with the law.

While not exceptionally fast with his Dragoon he could call himself fair. By Texas standards this meant he could draw, shoot at, and hit a man-sized target up to a range of twenty feet in one second; one needed to take at least a quarter of a second from that speed to be called fast. His French Creole and Comanche blood gave him a love of cold steel when in a fight and his mastery of the bowie knife was said to equal that of the knife's designer. In the use of the Winchester Model 1866 rifle he stood supreme and unchallenged, a master shot capable of almost fulfilling the somewhat exaggerated advertising claims the manufacturers made for their latest product.

All in all, Loncey Dalton Ysabel—Cuchilo, the Knife, to the Pehnane, Cabrito, which means Kid, among the border Mexicans who knew him in his smuggling days, or the Ysabel Kid from the Rio Grande to the Canadian border—possessed the means to be a real good friend, or just about as deadly an enemy as a man might ask to avoid.

Small wonder that Professor Hollenheimer, noted savant though he was, sat back and listened when the Ysabel Kid spoke on the subject of Indians in general and Comanche in particular.

"You said earlier that your grandfather was a chief of the Dog Soldier lodge, Kid," the professor said. "I didn't know that the Comanche had war lodges."

"Most of the bands didn't," admitted the Kid. "We got the idea from the Kiowa, most likely, us and them always being friendly. A boy got initiated into his pappy's lodge, which same I'm a Dog Soldier. We never went in for the lodge idea as strong as the other tribes, though. Sure, you sided a lodge brother, but not if doing it would be bad for the rest of the band."

Which differed from the practice of most Indian tribes, as Hollenheimer well knew. Among the Cheyenne and various subdivisions of the Sioux, one's lodge came first in all matters.

"Did you have lodge oaths?"

"Some, Professor. Only the revenge oath meant much to us, though."

"Could you repeat it to me?" Hollenheimer requested. "I speak some Comanche and would like to compare it with the vengeance oath of the Cheyenne and other tribes."

The Kid began to speak in the rather slow-tongued accent of the Pehnane Comanche. Even in the restful atmosphere of Ole Devil Hardin's near-sacred study, his small audience could sense the deep feeling of the guttural words. Yet none at that time realized just how different those same words would sound when spoken in true, serious, and deadly intent.

Curled comfortably in a chair on the left of the fireplace, small, black haired, and pretty, Betty Hardin listened with a tolerant smile. All she heard was a string of meaningless Comanche words. One day she would hear the Kid repeat the oath standing over the body of his murdered sweetheart and know the difference.*

The remaining occupants of the room were all men. Seated in the wheelchair that formed his home since he tried and failed to ride a magnificent, unbroken paint stallion,† Ole Devil Hardin, owner of the OD Connected ranch, looked as ramrod straight and nail hard as in the days when he commanded the Confederate Army of Arkansas. In those days he held a superior Yankee force at bay and might have played a vastly more important role in the conduct of the war had the South been able to supply him with more men, arms, and equipment. Now he sat in a wheelchair, lean, tanned, his sharp-featured face showing intelligence and breeding; a southern gen-

* Told in *Gunsmoke Thunder*.
† Told in *The Fastest Gun in Texas*.

tleman of the finest kind and a fighting man from soda to hock.

Sprawled at his ease facing Betty Hardin was a veritable giant of a man. Six feet three in height, with curly golden blond hair, an almost classically handsome face, which showed breeding and strength, great spreading shoulders, mighty biceps in evidence even as he sat relaxed, tapering down to a lean waist and powerful long legs, Mark Counter had the face of Apollo on the frame of Hercules. Something of a dandy dresser, his clothes set cowhand fashion in Texas just as the uniform he wore became the style adopted by the young bloods of the Confederate Cavalry. For all that, Mark could claim to be top hand with cattle. Although still young his great strength had become a legend and his prowess in a roughhouse brawl something discussed in awe wherever he displayed it. He might also have attained fame in matters *pistolero,* but his true ability in that line was hidden. Giant Mark Counter might be, but he stood in the shadow of the man many, including a number of the top names in the gun-fighting ranks, claimed to be the fastest, most deadly exponent of the art of combat gun-handling.

The man who overshadowed giant Mark Counter sat in a chair alongside Ole Devil Hardin, yet he seemed out of place in such company. Five feet six at most in height, he wore good quality range clothes, yet contrived to make them look as if some kind-hearted member of the ranch crew had handed them on to him, instead of their having been tailored to his fit. Dusty blond hair, rumpled and curly, framed a handsome, if not strikingly so, face. If one chanced to look a second time at that face and saw beyond the reposed ease, it held strength and showed a commanding aspect that only became apparent in time of need. A further study of his small frame gave a hint of a muscular development that compared favorably with that of Mark Counter, and had both men been the same height it would be hard to choose the finer figure.

At seventeen that small, insignificant man had been a captain in the Texas Light Cavalry and won considerable fame on the Arkansas battlefront as a military raider equal to John Singleton Mosby or Turner Ashby. Dusty Fog's methods changed the thinking of the U.S. Cavalry on light cavalry tactics in those days. At the head of a hard-riding company of Texans, he struck hard, fast, and unexpectedly shrewd blows that infuriated his enemies.

With the war ended Dusty Fog returned to the OD Connected. His uncle Ole Devil's injury put him in command of the great ranch and gave him the task, which he completed successfully, of riding the paint stallion. On a mission of vital importance into strife-torn Mexico, Dusty met up with Mark Counter and the Ysabel Kid. With their help he completed the mission and since then the three young Texans had become inseparable. They made a deadly efficient fighting team, one fast building a name throughout the range country.

Only just having returned from driving Ben Holland's Rocking H trail herd to Dodge City, in defiance of Wyatt Earp's order that it should not go there,* Dusty found another task awaiting him; one of some importance and that required careful handling.

The United States government wished to make peace with the Comanche nation and to persuade the stocky, hard-fighting masters of horseback warfare that they should move on to a reservation where some control might be exercised over them. To do so called for tact and diplomacy. Along with other prominent Texans who knew Indians in general and the Comanche in particular, Ole Devil Hardin aimed to ensure that nothing happened to spoil the chances for making a lasting peace.

Unable, due to his injury, to attend the meeting personally, Ole Devil had decided to send Dusty. Only the previous day word reached the ranch that Long Walker and

* Told in *Trail Boss*.

the other Pehnane leaders wished for the Kid to be present as their spokesman, to which Ole Devil raised no objections. Three members of the floating outfit would be starting the two-hundred-mile trip to Fort Sorrel the following morning. Mark Counter's father, a rich influential Big Bend rancher, telegraphed a request that his son be allowed to state the family views. Being a prewar friend Hollenheimer paid a courtesy visit to the OD Connected while on his way to the peace meeting and accepted the three Texans' offer to accompany them.

"What do you think're the chances of this meeting coming off, Lon?" asked Dusty after the conversation died down between the Kid and Hollenheimer.

"It might," the Kid replied. "Grandpappy Long Walker and the other old-man chiefs know they can't win in the end against the U.S. Army and reckon it's better to make peace now than wait until after the tribe's been licked all ways and *have* to move anyways."

"Do all the chiefs feel the same way?" Mark put in.

"Enough of them to give it a fair chance of coming off."

"How about Sidewinder?" Betty said quietly. "Will he be at the meeting?"

Over the past few years Sidewinder's name had risen high as the leading white-hater of the Texas Indians. Backed by a large band of bad-hat bucks, he raided, burned, looted, and murdered across the Lone Star State. Leaving a trail of carnage behind him Sidewinder did more than any other member of the Comanche nation to build up the opposition of many white people to any kind of peace with the Nemenuh.

"That's something the whole peace mission would like to know," Dusty guessed.

"Have you ever met him, Lon?" Betty asked, ignoring her cousin's comment.

"I don't know every Comanche," the Kid pointed out.

"One wouldn't forget that name easily," Hollenheimer

objected. "Although I realize he may not have had it for long."

"That's for sure," grinned the Kid. "I started out as 'Loncey,' but made Cuchilo my man-name. Not many Nemenuh go all through life with the same name. Funny, though, from what I've heard, Sidewinder is a Waw'ai and there's never before been a real name warrior come from among them."

"Waw'ai?" said Hollenheimer. "What band is that?"

"It means 'Wormy,' Professor. Most Comanche don't go a heap on the Waw'ai."

"Why?" Hollenheimer asked eagerly.

"We don't like the way they do some things."

"Such as?"

"Well, for one thing they let brother and sister hitch up," said the Kid.

"How do you mean, hitch up?" demanded the professor.

"Marry," Mark explained.

"Oh!" grunted Hollenheimer, and darted a glance at Betty.

To his surprise the professor saw a merry twinkle in the girl's eyes and no sign of embarrassment on her face. However, he did not feel they should continue discussing the seamy conduct of the Waw'ai band in the company of a young lady of good breeding. While Hollenheimer sought for a change of subject, Dusty supplied it.

"Do you reckon that Sidewinder will keep the peace after the other chiefs make it, Lon?"

"There's no reason why he should," answered the Kid. "Where all you white folks go wrong is that you will think an Indian acts your way. You think that a chief speaks for all the people."

"Don't they?"

"Most times they do, but there's nothing to force any man into doing something if he doesn't want to. He'll go along if he figures the chief's right. If he doesn't, he's free to do as he wants."

"So I've found among most tribes," confirmed Hollenheimer.

"If Sidewinder wants to come in, he'll do it," the Kid went on. "If not—"

"The U.S. Army will fetch him in," Ole Devil interrupted.

"They'll try to, sir," corrected the Kid. "Only, if they go after him and miss out, they've made his medicine stronger and that'll sway folks who aren't sure about making peace."

"It's as bad as that?" asked Betty.

"Worse," the Kid replied. "Take it this way, Betty gal. The Comanche are top men among the Texas Indians. If they make peace, the Kiowa, Kaddo, Waco, and Wichita chiefs'll figure there's no hope for them to go on fighting and they'll come in. If the Comanche don't make peace, then the other tribes won't."

The conversation continued for a time on more general lines. At last Hollenheimer asked to be excused.

"Reckon I'll take a walk down to the corral," the Kid drawled.

"I'll come along with you," Betty remarked, rising from her chair. "I want to look in on that dun mare in the barn. She ought to foal tonight."

"I'm for bed," Dusty stated.

"And me," drawled Mark, stretching to his full height. "Give that cross-grained white goat a kiss for me, Lon."

"I hope that you meant Lon's horse Shadow, Mark Counter," said Betty in a threatening manner.

"He didn't, Betty gal," grinned the Kid. "You hand him his needings."

"I would," the girl assured him. "But Dusty needs him to tote the heavy weights in the morning."

"He never misses going to see that hoss afore he beds down," Mark said as the library door closed. "I reckon

Lon thinks it's not safe to have Shadow down in the corral instead of standing outside the house door."

"He certainly knows Indians," Hollenheimer remarked.

"There are times when Lon *is* an Indian," Dusty drawled. "Or so near that it doesn't matter."

CHAPTER TWO

DANGER IN THE DARKNESS

On leaving the library Betty and the Kid found a small smiling man of obvious Oriental birth approaching them. Small he might be, but, like Dusty, he gave the impression of great strength. Dressed in a neat white tunic and trousers with sandals on his feet, the man might be young or old, one could not tell by looking at him. He was Tommy Okasi, Ole Devil's personal servant. Popular conception among the ranch hands called Tommy Okasi Chinese; a point he hotly denied, claiming to come from some place called Nippon.

Brought from Japan by Commander Perry's expedition, Tommy took service with Ole Devil Hardin when they met in New Orleans. The little man gave his master loyalty and yet was not servile in any way. Many a newcomer among the cowhands, used to the meek Chinese of the frontier towns, learned quickly and painfully that it did not pay to try the same kind of games with Ole Devil's servant. Tommy Okasi possessed a very thorough knowledge of certain fighting arts little known outside the country of his birth and which gave him a considerable advantage over bigger, stronger men.

"Is Devil-san ready for going to bed?" Tommy asked.

"He is," Betty stated definitely. "Tell him I said so."

After Ole Devil, Tommy gave his loyalty to Betty and Dusty. They alone of the Fog, Hardin, and Blaze clan received tuition in the ancient Japanese fighting arts of jujitsu and karate from the little man, and he accepted orders only from them in his master's absence.

"I tell him," Tommy said and entered the gun-decorated room.

While Betty spoke with Tommy Okasi, the Kid walked across the hall and took his gun belt from where it hung by the front door. There would be little chance of his needing either the Dragoon or bowie knife on the safe home range of the OD Connected, but he knew that if the need arose there would be no time to start thinking of running back to the house and collecting them.

Expecting a pedigree mare to foal that night Betty wore a tartan shirt, Levi's pants, and moccasins instead of the dress she usually adopted when entertaining guests. She walked toward the door, seeing nothing out of the ordinary in the Kid strapping on his gun belt. Most of her life had been spent on the Texas range, and knowing most of the top names of the fast-draw fraternity, she could understand and heartily approve of his actions.

"I hope everything goes off smoothly, Lon," she remarked as they left the house and crossed the porch.

"And me—I think."

"Aren't you sure it will?"

"Grandpappy Long Walker wants peace," the Kid said. "And he'll keep his word once he makes it, as long as the white folks do the same and play square with him."

"The Comanche will be given a decent piece of land—" Betty began.

"Which was once a little bit of what they owned before the white men came," the Kid interrupted. "Comancheria used to cover from the Rio Grande, along the Pecos up into Colorado and Kansas, right over to beyond Fort Sill."

"And you took most of that from the weaker, less warlike tribes," Betty pointed out. "You've told me so yourself."

A faint grin came to the Kid's face, his teeth gleaming white in the darkness of the night. "Never could stand a gal who remembered all the fool things I told her. You're right, the Nemenuh took what they wanted and now the white men are doing it back to us. Only, it'll be hard for a Comanche to stay inside the boundary of a reservation."

"I suppose so," Betty sighed.

"When I was a button, the Pehnane roamed headwaters of the Central Texas rivers and the Cross Timbers country from the Pecos to Fort Phantom Hill. If the hunting was poor one place, we just upped stakes and moved to another. If we pull off this treaty, the Pehnane, Kweharehnuh, Detsanawyehka, Yamparikuh, Tanima, and Waw'ai bands will all be held on the one reservation. In a few years at most all the game'll be gone, the hoss herds'll eat the grass down to bare roots. There'll be no war or raiding for the young men. Nothing of the old ways'll be left."

"You liked the old ways?" It was more of a statement than a question.

"They were fine—"

"For the Comanche," Betty put in. "But not so good for the folks who lived near to them."

"Likely not," admitted the Kid. "We raided for hosses and loot—I was too young to do it—and they did the same back on us, but there was never any real bad fuss between the different Comanche bands."

"Didn't you have feuds?"

"Some. Mostly, though, they'd be between pure Comanches and prisoners adopted into the tribe. You'd fight with somebody, but never steal from them."

"Weren't there any thieves among the Comanche?"

"Not for long. Happen a man was caught stealing from another Nemenuh, they'd cut off his right hand. If he did it again, they'd chop off the left. You might see a feller with one hand, but never one who'd lost them both."

"That sounds like pretty rough justice," Betty said.

"It worked and sure discouraged thieves," drawled the Kid. "Which same they had to be discouraged, there's no way you can lock up a tepee. I'll never forget the first time I saw a white settlement. I'd be rising twelve at the time and I wondered how the hell they managed to move such big wood houses."

While talking they walked side by side toward the big corrals that stood some distance from the house. Betty glanced at the tall young man and gave a little sigh. Often before she had heard the Kid speak of his early life among the Pehnane, but not in that wistful manner. Clearly he felt regret at the end of what must have been a marvelously free way of life.

Betty could sympathize with the Kid in his present position. All too well he knew what reservation life would be like. Instead of hunting buffalo, deer, or elk for their food, the Comanche would be dependent on supplies from the agent in charge of their reservation. All too often such men thought only of their own profit and sold most of the Indians' rations. The limited range available would not support the Comanches' huge horse herds, and to the Nemenuh horses were a sign of wealth or social standing.

Yet the Kid realized the futility of resistance. During the Civil War many new and improved ways of killing large numbers of human beings had been perfected—the Gatling gun, and light, quick-firing breach-loading artillery to name but two. Against such weapons the Comanche, great horse-fighters though they might be, could not hope to survive for long. So the Kid must advise his grandfather and the other chiefs to accept the white man's offer. Betty prayed that Dusty, Mark, and the other influential Texans attending the meeting could force a decent, honorable settlement with the eastern politicians responsible for making the treaty.

Suddenly, appearing to rise out of the very ground, two figures loomed before the Kid and Betty, bringing them out of their respective thought-trains with a jolt. While the ranch's crew were no different from other cowhands in their love of playing practical jokes, neither

Betty nor the Kid even began to think the appearance heralded the start of a piece of playful, harmless fooling. Steel glinted in the dull starlight and no cowhand would be stupid enough to play games holding knives in their hands.

For once in his life the Kid's inborn alertness, made more keen by his childhood training, almost failed him in the matter of detecting a hostile presence. Like Betty he had been thinking of his people's future; no matter that now folks regarded him as a Texan of Texans, he still thought of himself as a Pehnane Comanche. So the sudden appearance of the two men came as a surprise that slammed him out of his reverie. At another time, when less engrossed, he would have located the pair far sooner. A mixed stink of stale human sweat and rancid antelope grease came clearly to his nostrils, giving warning and recalling something told to him by his maternal grandfather during a boyhood lesson on Comanche ways.

Even as the thought clicked home, the Kid's brain raced in its assessing of the situation. Realizing that his knife would not serve at such a moment—before he could deal with one attacker the other was sure to get him—the Kid reached for his old Dragoon Colt. His right hand twisted palm outward and curled around the familiar walnut grips, raising the four pound, one ounce weight from the carefully contoured holster. No other method of carrying a Dragoon Colt offered such ease of removal as the low cavalry-draw rig such as the Kid used. It allowed the thumb to curl around the hammer, and the barrel come into line, with the minimum of movement. At such a moment every movement saved paid its dividend by keeping the one making the draw alive.

While drawing with his right hand he used the left to shove Betty aside. In doing so the Kid hoped to bring both attackers down on him. Too late he saw that one of the men swung in the girl's direction. At that late moment the Kid could not hope to change his point of aim. If it came to a point, he did not need to aim with the man so close. Removing his thumb from the hammer, having already pressed the trigger as soon as the Colt left its holster and lined away from him, the Kid shot his attacker. Driven by the full force of forty grains of prime du Pont black powder, a round ball packed a punch unequaled in any handgun of the day. It not only halted the charging attacker but flung him backward and from his feet as it smashed into his chest.

Staggering from the Kid's push Betty saw her danger. An eastern miss under such conditions might have done no more than scream and swoon, but Betty Hardin had been born and raised in frontier Texas. While not underestimating the danger she prepared to meet it.

The second man bore down on Betty. Seeing the way she dressed, he took her for a man and had sufficient respect for a Texas ride-plenty's fighting prowess to figure that even such a small one could be deadly dangerous. So he left dealing with the Kid to his companion and made for the girl. Holding his knife Indian fashion, with the blade extending below the hand—as opposed to the more efficient method of gripping it so the thumb and forefinger touched the quillons of the guard—he launched a savage downward chop aimed at the side of the girl's neck.

Catching her balance and coming to a halt Betty threw all her weight on to her left leg. Pivoting around she drew up her knee toward her chest and tilted her torso under the arc of the knife slash. Taken off balance her assailant could not halt his advance or save himself. By swinging her raised leg in an outward circle, Betty sent her foot driving forward to land with sickening force in the pit of the man's stomach. It was not the wild kick of a frightened girl, but one of the devastatingly effective karate techniques learned from Tommy Okasi.

Breath gushed from the man's lips as the kick landed

and he doubled over, letting the knife fall from his hands as he clutched at his stomach. As he staggered by Betty, winded and all but helpless, she turned and delivered a stamping kick to the back of his left leg, buckling it under him and bringing him crashing to the ground.

Whirling around, the Kid found that he would not need his gun to protect Betty. He sprang forward, landing so as to ram his knee into the small of the second man's back. Knowing something of the Kid's nature when roused, Betty yelled a warning to him.

"Take him alive, Lon!"

Up rose the Kid's right arm and drove downward to smash the bottom of the Dragoon's butt against the man's skull. Instantly the other's struggles ended and he went limp.

In the house Dusty and Mark heard the sound of the shot. They stood in the hall with Hollenheimer and Ole Devil, having been on the point of going upstairs to their rooms. Without wasting a second the two young men turned and ran toward the main door. Dusty arrived first, sliding one of his bone-handled 1860 Army Colts from its holster in passing and jerking open the door. Drawing the ivory-handled Army Colt from the right holster of his belt, Mark followed Dusty out on to the porch and sprang across it on his friend's heels.

"What's happening?" Hollenheimer asked.

"We'll go take a look." Ole Devil replied, and told Tommy Okasi to take him to the front door.

"Some dogs you've got, gal," grunted the Kid, coming to his feet as Dusty and Mark burst out of the house.

"Uncle Hondo took them over to Cousin Buck's north range after that cougar that's been living on Double B beef," Betty replied, leaping to the defense of her highly prized quartet of bluetick big-game hounds.

The shot brought men from the bunkhouse as well as the main building. One of the cowhands let out a yell and pointed toward the ranch house, making both Betty and the Kid forget about the blueticks that would have prevented the attackers approaching undetected had they been in their usual place on the porch.

What attracted the cowhands' attention was the sight of an all-but-naked figure darting along the porch toward the main doors. Knife in hand the man on the porch made for where Tommy Okasi was pushing Ole Devil's wheelchair out of the door.

Not only Betty and the Kid heard the cowhand's warning. Dusty skidded into a turning halt. Facing the house he went instantly into a gunfighter's crouch and lined his gun from waist high. Twice Dusty fired, cocking the Colt on its recoil and sending the lead by instinctive alignment. Even as Tommy Okasi sprang before Ole Devil, ready to protect his master, Dusty heard the distinctive *whomp!* of lead striking human flesh. The attacker reeled, struck the wall, and slid down it to the porch's floor.

"Any more of them?" Mark called, holding his Colt ready for use.

"I don't reckon so," the Kid answered.

"Get a lamp over here!" Dusty called. "Look around some, Lon, Billy Jack."

"Yo!" came the cavalry-inspired answer from the cowhand named.

Returning to the porch Dusty looked at the man he had shot. Naked but for a brief breechclout, body glistening with the same kind of grease that gave the Kid a warning, a tallish, lean Indian lay dying at Dusty's feet. Dying or not Dusty took no chances and kicked away the razor-sharp Green River knife dropped by the man.

"What the hell?" mused the small Texan; for it had been several years since Indians had made trouble on the OD Connected range.

In the light of a lamp brought from the bunkhouse, Mark stood looking down at the other two attackers. Both were Indians in the same state of undress as the one on the porch. Before the blond giant could form any impressions, he saw that Betty's assailant showed signs of recovery and so told one of the cowhands to fetch a rope from the bunkhouse.

"What tribe is he from, Dusty?" Hollenheimer asked.

"I'm not sure," Dusty replied. "Reckon I'd best go and see what's doing, sir."

"It'd be best," Ole Devil agreed.

By the time Dusty joined Mark and his cousin, the Kid had returned from making a quick scout of the area.

"Nothing," the dark youngster reported. "I don't reckon there're anymore of them around." He dropped to his knee by the groaning Indian and turned the man face upward. "A Waw'ai!" he growled. "It's one of their games, rubbing the body with antelope grease when they go out on a scalp-lifting raid."

"But the nearest Waw'ai country's—" Mark began.

"Yeah, I know," interrupted the Kid. "It's a good three hundred miles from here. But this bunch are Waw'ais, or I've never seen one."

At that moment one of the cowhands came up with a rope and Mark took it. Kneeling at the Kid's side Mark quickly secured the groaning Indian's wrists with the rope. With that done Mark rose and lifted the man erect and held him upright as if the other weighed no more than a baby.

"Let's take him down to the barn and make talk," suggested the Kid.

"Not the barn," Betty objected. "I don't want that mare disturbed."

"Use the store cabin," Dusty told the Kid, and looked at the assembled cowhands. "Billy Jack, get the bodies moved. You'd best leave them in the forge until we can have pappy over to look at them."

Being country sheriff Dusty's father would want to examine the bodies when he heard of the attempted murders. The tall, gangling, miserable-looking cowhand who rode as Dusty's very able sergeant major during the war nodded and gave the necessary orders. Leaving the removal of the bodies in Billy Jack's hands, Dusty turned to his cousin.

"You'd best go to bed, Betty," he said.

Obediently the girl turned and walked toward the house. There were times when she laid down the law in no uncertain manner and she ruled the house firmly, but Betty knew better than stand arguing when Dusty's voice held that quiet, deadly serious note.

"What's happening, Dusty?" Hollenheimer asked, joining the small Texan.

"We're just now going to find out," Dusty replied, and suddenly he ceased to be a small, insignificant figure. In a strange way he appeared to grow until he gave the impression of towering over big Mark Counter even.

"How?"

"Any way we have to."

"Can I come along?"

"It might be better if you didn't, Professor," Dusty warned. "There's more than just a chance raid to this. So I aim to find out what's behind it and the Indian might not want to tell me."

"I assure you that I don't want to come along out of idle or morbid curiosity," Hollenheimer replied. "And I promise that I won't interfere in any way."

"All right, Professor," Dusty said. "You can come along. But understand *now* that I'll hold you to your promise."

Hollenheimer formed some idea of what had made Dusty a cavalry captain at seventeen and the peace officer who tamed a wild Montana mining town after three less able men had died trying* as he watched the small Texan. Quietly, yet in a manner that showed he expected instant and unquestioning obedience, Dusty told the ranch crew not assisting Billy Jack to return to the bunkhouse. Cowhands were not noted for mild obedi-

---

* Told in *Quiet Town*.

ence or accepting a man as their boss merely because he happened to be related to the owner of the ranch. Yet not one of them raised any objections to doing as Dusty ordered. Talking among themselves the cowhands walked away in the direction of the bunkhouse.

Half carrying the Waw'ai, Mark headed for the store cabin and the Kid walked at his side. Neither spoke, but both knew that they might be involved in something unpleasant before very long.

Before following his friends Dusty returned to the porch. Ole Devil sat at the door, showing some impatience.

"Well, Dustine?" growled the rancher.

"They're Waw'ai Comanches according to Lon, sir," Dusty replied. "Three of them. We only managed to take one alive."

"This isn't Waw'ai country, and never was," commented Ole Devil.

"Yes, sir," agreed Dusty. "I'm going to ask the one we took alive about that."

"Let me know what you learn," Ole Devil ordered.

"I'll do just that, sir," promised Dusty.

Hollenheimer stood waiting for Dusty and accompanied the small Texan toward the store cabin.

"How do you propose to get answers, Dusty?" he asked.

A cold set mask replaced Dusty's usual easygoing expression. "Any way I have to use, Professor," the small Texan said.

CHAPTER THREE

NAMES FROM THE PAST

With Hollenheimer following on his heels Dusty entered the small cabin selected as the best place in which to interrogate the Waw'ai prisoner. The Kid had brought along a lamp and hung it from a hook fitted into the roof for that purpose. As Dusty and the professor entered, the other two Texans put the final touch, to fastening the Waw'ai to the wall.

Although called a store cabin the building served mainly as a workshop for saddlery repair. Harness, spare saddles, bridles, and other horse equipment lay around the single room. In its center stood a stout table, and two heavy benches were set against the walls. Looking around him Hollenheimer saw a number of items that might serve as instruments of torture, although their true purpose was the repair or making of leatherwork. Tearing his eyes from the stout needles and short, sharp, curved-bladed knives, he looked at the prisoner.

Clearly Mark and the Kid had wasted no time on their arrival. Already the Waw'ai stood with his back to the wall, arms drawn up and apart with ropes secured to pegs in the wall and his legs held apart, fastened to the workbenches. Tied in such a position by experts in the use of ropes, the Indian could barely move.

Hollenheimer studied the Indian with some interest. Most Comanches tended to be short to medium in height, with stocky, robust bodies. Although showing a wiry, muscular development, the Waw'ai was tall and slim. He had the normal straight black hair of all Indians and the slightly Mongoloid features of the Comanche. All he wore was the smallest breechclout Hollenheimer had ever seen, and his body glistened in the lamp's light. If he felt afraid, the Waw'ai did not show it, but scowled defiantly at his captors.

"He said anything yet?" asked Dusty.

"Only one thing," the Kid replied, lips twisted in a wolf-savage grin. "I won't tell you what."

"Ask him why he came here," Dusty ordered.

Turning back to the Waw'ai the Kid repeated Dusty's question in Comanche. At first the Indian made no reply, then he grunted something.

"He allows they came to steal horses," interpreted the Kid, then swung back to the prisoner. "That's a lie. No Waw'ai ever raided over the ridge behind his village. You came here to kill me."

Only a grunt left the Waw'ai's lips and he hung his head in a surly manner. Mark shoved the man's head back, forcing him to look straight ahead. Taking out his knife the Kid held it before the Waw'ai's eyes and then lowered it to the level of the breechclout.

"Tell me who sent you, or I'll make you half a man," he growled.

For a moment fear flickered in the Waw'ai's dark eyes and the Kid thought his threat might work. Then the Indian stiffened his features into a cold, expressionless mask.

"Strike, Pehnane dog-eater!" he snarled.

"Aiee, Namae'enuh!"* said the Kid, using another name for the Waw'ai. "Would you go back to your people and not be able to make children with your sister?"

* Namae'enuh: Put politely it means They-who-have-incestuous-intercourse.

"Strike, don't talk!" the Waw'ai spat back after a brief pause.

Watching the Kid at that moment, Hollenheimer wondered how he ever thought the other looked young and innocent. Nothing in the Kid's cold Dog Soldier's mask of a face led the professor to believe he would hesitate before castrating the prisoner. Nor did there seem to be any chance of Dusty or Mark making a move to prevent it happening. Suddenly Hollenheimer's mouth felt rather dry and he ran his tongue tip over parched lips, wondering what he ought to do.

However, the Kid understood Indians far better than Hollenheimer, academic knowledge and international reputation notwithstanding, ever could. All too well the Kid knew how an Indian would stand up to pain. Mere torture could not bring out the required answers. No Comanche would doubt that another Nemenuh aimed to carry out a threat of torture, yet the Waw'ai seemed resigned to the hideous fate of losing his manhood. That meant the Waw'ai must have some strong *puha*, medicine power, behind him. The Kid knew the futility of using ordinary methods when dealing with the sacred state of *puha*. Neither the threat nor actuality of castration would make the prisoner talk.

"I see you are a brave man," he said. "If you tell me why you came and who sent you, I will let you go free."

"And what will your white friends do?" asked the Waw'ai.

"This is the one called Magic Hands," replied the Kid, indicating Dusty. "He who came to the big council when the white men fought among themselves and broke the medicine of the Devil Gun."

During the war a pair of fanatical Union supporters took an Agar coffee mill machine gun to a council of Indian tribes in North Texas and hoped to use it as an inducement to send the tribes on the warpath. On learning of the plot Dusty led a small party of men, including the Kid's father, to the council and ruined the insane plot.* In doing so he gained quite a reputation among the Texas Indians, and the Kid could see that the Waw'ai was impressed at coming face to face with the fabled Magic Hands; who had such courage that he threw aside his revolvers when stood before the Devil Gun so as to make its owners fight him.

"Magic Hands would keep his word," admitted the Waw'ai. "But if I speak, the Death Bringer's *puha* will kill me."

"It's medicine business, Dusty," the Kid explained, turning to his waiting friends. "Unless we can break it, he'll not talk."

"Then we'll have to break it," Dusty answered. "Those three jaspers came here to kill you, and likely Uncle Devil. I aim to find out why and who sent them."

"I could work on him," the Kid said. "But he'll not talk with a death curse hanging over him."

"Perhaps I can help," Hollenheimer put in, moving forward from his place by the door.

Hearing the voice the Waw'ai looked for the first time away from the grim-faced trio of Texans. He stared with some interest and surprise at the tall, stately figure of the noted eastern savant, gazing at Hollenheimer's head with special attentiveness.

During his last lecture tour in England, Hollenheimer had mingled with upper-class sportsmen and adopted their style of leisure wear. Even on his visit to the OD Connected he chose to wear a dark burgundy smoking jacket and a red fez decorated in black silk with various cabalistic signs. Such a style of dress had attracted comment among the ranch crew and certainly the Waw'ai, his knowledge of white men limited to soldiers and native Texans, never saw its like. Studying the crescent moon and five-pointed star motif of the fez's decoration, the

* Told in *The Devil Gun.*

27

Waw'ai wondered what kind of white man fate had thrown him into contact with.

"How do you mean, Professor?" asked Dusty, while the Kid looked from the Waw'ai to Hollenheimer's fez and back.

"I've found that displaying pseudomagical powers often has a most salutary effect upon the Indian," Hollenheimer explained.

"How about making that so a half-smart li'l Texas boy like me can follow it?" requested the Kid.

"I'm somewhat skilled at sleight-of-hand," Hollenheimer answered. "Learned in college originally, as a means of entertainment during fraternity dinners rather than with any serious intention. However, it came in most useful in gaining the confidence of the Indian, when used in conjunction with a demonstration of some easily transported scientific development that smacked of the supernatural to the uncultured braves."

"Which same, we're a mite short on scientific developments down here on the OD Connected," Dusty drawled, guessing what the other had in mind.

"I brought one of the latest model microscopes back from England; it's in my trunk," Hollenheimer told him. "Would that work, do you think?"

"It'd do for a start," the Kid admitted when Dusty explained the purpose of a microscope.

"Then I could perform some sleight-of-hand," Hollenheimer went on, warming to the idea; especially as it might prevent the need for using physical torture. "Pull a bullet out of midair, or a coin from his ear."

"Which same any halfway good Nemenuh witchman or -woman can do?" drawled the Kid. "No, sir. Happen you aim to make him think you're a top medicine man who's strong enough to break the death curse, you'll have to do a whole heap better than that."

"Happen the microscope works," Dusty drawled, "I've

an idea that'll make this hombre think he's run across the top medicine man of the whole white race."

"What's that?" asked Mark.

"Go get the microscope," Dusty told him, ignoring the question.

"It's packed in a polished wooden box in my trunk, Mark," Hollenheimer went on. "Tommy will find it for you if you ask him."

"Do that," Dusty said. "And ask Uncle Devil if he'll let Tommy come back here with you. Tell him it's mighty important."

"Sure," Mark answered, and left without further talk.

"You start telling that Waw'ai what a right fine medicine man the professor is, Lon," Dusty continued. "Lay it on good and thick."

"Why, sure," grinned the Kid, having such faith in the small Texan that he needed no further instructions or explanation. "Start up some of your magic, Professor, so's he can see that I'm not fooling."

Although the Waw'ai tended to scoff and stated that he had never heard of the white people having medicine men, he stared at Hollenheimer, who nonchalantly reached an apparently empty hand into the air and produced a silver dollar between his fingertips. Give the professor his due, no matter what motive lay behind his acquiring a knowledge of sleight-of-hand, he learned real well. Working with only the items from his pockets, he performed a series of highly diverting tricks. Dusty and the Kid watched with interest, seeing that the Waw'ai gave Hollenheimer his attention without being overimpressed.

Mark returned with Tommy Okasi, who carried the microscope box and set it on the table. Walking over, Hollenheimer opened the box, took out, and set up the microscope. Then he handed Mark one of the slides and told the blond giant to take it outside, then place a couple of spots of water, from the rain-filled barrel against the side of the building, onto it. While Mark went to obey, Hollenheimer gave the Kid his instructions.

"This white medicine man has great *puha*," the Kid informed the Waw'ai.

"I haven't seen it yet," the Indian sniffed.

"Soon you will," promised the Kid, voice holding a threatening note.

When Mark reentered the cabin, Hollenheimer took the slide from him and carried it to where the Waw'ai stood. Holding the slide between the tips of his fingers, Hollenheimer raised it to before the Indian's eyes.

"What do you see?" he asked, speaking Comanche.

"A small piece of white man's glass," answered the Waw'ai, and showed surprise at hearing his native tongue come from the strangely dressed white man.

"Nothing more?"

"It is only a small piece of glass, with a little water on it."

"You do not see things moving in the water?"

"There could be nothing in such a tiny spot," scoffed the Waw'ai.

"Bring him to the table," ordered Hollenheimer, and backed away, keeping the slide in plain view all the time.

While guessing that Hollenheimer had aroused their prisoner's interest, Dusty did not intend to take chances. After unfastening the Waw'ai's legs, but before freeing his arms, Dusty hobbled his ankles in such a manner that he could walk but not make any sudden moves.

Hollenheimer made sure that the Waw'ai would receive the full benefit of a modern scientific wonder, placing the slide into position and focusing the microscope while the freeing of the Indian took place. On the man being brought to the table, Hollenheimer removed the slide from beneath the lens and repeated his question. Again the Waw'ai insisted that he saw only a piece of glass with a spot of water on it. Then Hollenheimer let the Indian peer through the microscope without placing the slide into position. Following Hollenheimer's instructions the Indian looked.

"I see nothing," said the Waw'ai a shade uneasily, wondering how such a large circle of bright light could be at the bottom of the narrow tube.

"Then look again!" boomed Hollenheimer, and with a flourish many a professional stage magician might have envied, put the slide into position.

More curious than interested, the Waw'ai bent once more over the microscope and squinted into the eyepiece. Instantly his body stiffened and he let out a yell. No longer did he see a bright light, but a murky circle in which hideous shapes moved, writhed, and twisted. Jerking backward, disregarding the hobbles on his ankles, the Indian sat down hard on his rump. Hollenheimer removed the slide and held it toward the horrified face of the Indian, causing him to try to shuffle back across the floor.

"Now do you believe?" demanded the Kid.

"Aiee!" exclaimed the Waw'ai. "He has much *puha."*

"He is the greatest medicine man of the white people," the Kid stated, for Dusty had explained the rest of the scheme while Hollenheimer introduced the Indian to the wonders of the microscope. "This medicine man can give powers that makes a man beyond pain and of great strength."

"That I have not seen," the Waw'ai said, but his voice showed uncertainty.

"See that small yellow one?" asked the Kid, pointing to Tommy. "The medicine man gave him *puha* so that he can break wood with his bare hands or feet."

"I would like to see such *puha,"* the Waw'ai stated.

"You will," the Kid promised.

Quickly, with Hollenheimer listening, Dusty told Tommy Okasi what he wanted done, and the small Oriental nodded. Tommy understood the gravity of the situation and realized that he must play a vital part in Dusty's plan. So he raised no objection to giving a demonstration of the *tameshiwari* technique of karate. Darting glances around the room Tommy located what he required. Following the direction of Tommy's gaze Dusty walked over, picked up a broom from where it leaned in the corner, and kicked its head from the handle. With the handle in his hands he went to where the Kid helped the Waw'ai up from the floor.

"Tell him to break this with his bare hands, Lon," Dusty said, holding out the handle.

"No man, not even the big one there, could do that," stated the Waw'ai, nodding to Mark.

"The small yellow man can—if he has the medicine man's *puha*," replied the Kid. "We will show you."

Knowing what would be needed, Mark picked up two wooden blocks and set them about eighteen inches apart on the tabletop. Hollenheimer made impressive passes with his hands around Tommy and chanted a string of Latin words, giving the Waw'ai the idea that he conferred *puha* upon the small Oriental. Meanwhile Dusty laid the broom handle across the blocks and gripped one end of it, Mark taking hold of the other end so as to hold it firmly in place.

With the scene set Tommy walked toward the table. To obtain the necessary concentration of strength at the point of impact, Tommy needed to coordinate his breathing, timing, and speed with the power of his entire body. Standing relaxed, toes gripping the floor—he had removed his sandals on hearing what Dusty wanted—Tommy inhaled deeply through his nose and his eyes fixed on the broom handle with calculating intensity. Then he tensed, going into the *fudotachi* fighting stance, legs apart and bent, right arm extended with the hand held in the *tegatana* hand-sword position. Up whipped the right arm and drove down again, moving almost too fast for the eye to follow.

"Kiai!" Tommy shouted as the heel of his hand crashed

on to the center of that part of the broom handle between the two blocks.

Dusty and Mark felt the sudden jolt, then the wood cracked, splintered, and broke. A startled exclamation burst from Hollenheimer, having never seen the deadly *tameshiwari* method of breaking wood with the bare hands. Luckily the Waw'ai was too amazed to notice that the white "medicine man" seemed remarkably surprised at the effect of his own *puha*.

Without giving any sign of noticing the effect his demonstration had on the Indian, Tommy turned and walked across the room. Again he paused to gather his full power, then gave the traditional spiritual cry of *"Kiai!"* and delivered a *yoko kekomi* side-thrusting kick that drove his foot through the planks of the wall. The move happened so swiftly that the Waw'ai could hardly believe his eyes and Hollenheimer's mouth dropped open as he stared at the jagged hole in what had been solid timber.

"Now do you believe me?" asked the Kid of the staring Waw'ai.

Dragging his eyes from the shattered plank the Indian nodded. "I believe. No Nemenuh medicine man could give such *puha.*"

"The white witchman can save you from any death curse," the Kid pointed out. "So if you tell us what we want to know, you can go free and no harm will come to you for doing it."

Only for a moment did the Waw'ai hesitate. Any nation that could produce the marvels which the white men possessed, like repeating rifles, revolvers, steel knives and arrowheads, must have medicine men of great power. From what he had just witnessed, those same medicine men were capable of producing miraculous results on human beings. More than one Comanche medicine man claimed to have a power to protect a brave from injury, but all failed when put to the acid test. Yet the white man's *puha* worked. That broken broom handle and shattered wall gave proof of its effectiveness.

Although superstitious, the Waw'ai was no fool. He knew that a refusal to answer would mean a long, painful session of torture to make him tell and most likely death at the end no matter what happened. Only fear of the Death Bringer's curse held him from cooperating, and now he could see a way to avoid it.

"If I speak, the white medicine man will give me his *puha* and I can go free?" he asked.

"I have said it," the Kid replied.

"You say it on the sun curse?" demanded the Waw'ai.

"If you tell us all we ask, you can go free," the Kid promised, and drew himself up erect. "Sun, father, you heard me say it. Earth, mother, you heard me say it. Do not let me live another season if I speak with forked a tongue."

Satisfaction showed on the Waw'ai's face as the Kid spoke the words of the sun curse. No Nemenuh of Cuchilo's birth and upbringing would repeat the sacred oath unless he meant it.

"The Death Bringer sent us to kill you, Cuchilo. Also the old one called Diablo Viejo."

"That's Ole Devil," the Kid told his white audience; mainly for Hollenheimer's benefit. He turned back to the Waw'ai. "Why were you to kill us?"

"I do not know," the man admitted. "When the Death Bringer orders, only a fool, and one soon to be dead, refuses to obey."

"Who is the Death Bringer?" Hollenheimer put in.

And nearly spoiled everything. The Waw'ai showed his surprise that such a great medicine man would be so ignorant.

"She is the mother of Sidewinder and a great witch-woman," he said.

"Is she a Waw'ai?" the Kid asked, hoping that Hollenheimer would have enough sense to keep quiet.

"Yes," the Indian replied.

"Was she born into the Waw'ai?"

"No. She and her son came to us many seasons ago. At first we thought to kill them both, for she was Mexican and her son lame from a knife wound so badly none expected him to walk again."

"Great day in the morning!" the Kid breathed, all ordinary oaths being inadequate for his feelings at the news.

"The wound healed and the woman became a great witch. Her son rose to be a warbonnet chief, a mighty raider and taker of many scalps," the Waw'ai went on, not understanding the Kid's exclamation or interest. "She says we must not make peace with the white man, that the council they call is a trick."

"What's up, Lon?" Mark asked, seeing the strained expression on the Kid's face.

"When I told you I didn't know Sidewinder," the Kid replied in hardly more than a whisper, "I was wrong. I know him real good."

"Who is he?" asked Dusty. "And who's the Death Bringer?"

"She's a Mexican prisoner who was adopted into the Pehnane. They called her Fire Dancer, and she had a son. He got the name No Father on account of pappy killing his old man the day I was born."

"So you know Sidewinder then," Hollenheimer said.

"I know him, all right," agreed the Kid. "It was my knife that crippled him and the next time we meet, one of us is going to die."

CHAPTER FOUR

THE DEATH BRINGER'S ORDERS

While Dusty and the others might have liked to hear more about the Kid's reason for intending to kill No Father, or Sidewinder, as he was now known, they knew they could waste no time asking about it. By showing ignorance of the Death Bringer's identity, Hollenheimer could have weakened the Waw'ai's faith in his spiritual powers. At any moment the Indian might realize that he had been tricked and no demonstrations of Tommy's *tameshiwari* powers, displays of other scientific wonders, or the most painful physical tortures—would elicit further details from the Waw'ai.

"Ask him what other men were sent out," Dusty told the Kid, with a sinking feeling that he already knew the answer and could even guess at the identity of the proposed victims.

So far doubt had not crept too deeply into the Waw'ai's head. He glanced at the hole in the wall, then toward the microscope and concluded that the white medicine man might be jealous of the Death Bringer's powers and so pretended not to know her.

"We were only one of the parties she sent out," he replied when the Kid passed on Dusty's question. "Other brave-hearts also went to kill."

Seeing Hollenheimer open his mouth to ask a question, Dusty swung around to put his back to the Waw'ai and face the savant.

"So help me, Professor," he hissed, "if you ask another fool question, I'll see if I can bring off one of Tommy's stunts on you."

While a man of some considerable importance and used to respect, Hollenheimer did not regard himself as a demigod or expect everybody to worship at his feet. He realized that only a colossal blunder on his part would cause Dusty to address him in such a manner and a moment's thought told him where he had gone wrong. So he held back from repeating the mistake and allowed the Kid to continue with the questioning.

"All right," said the Kid, ignoring the interruption. "Who are those to die?"

Even as the Kid asked the question, a man walked toward his death.

The Reverend Miles Boardwell strolled through the darkness toward his home on the outskirts of Mound Prairie, Anderson County. A tall, stalwart man of commanding appearance, the reverend was a popular figure in his hometown and the surrounding district; liked and respected despite his expressed views on the subject of fair play and decent treatment for the Indians. Any parson who made his sermons short but interesting, regarded moderate drinking and gambling as acceptable human weaknesses, and could forget his cloth during the week to the extent of going hunting or fishing with his parishioners, must be excused his one minor idiosyncrasy—especially in an area long removed from Indian depredations. So, although a few of the staider souls whispered that he should not associate himself with such a controversial issue, nobody raised any objections to his decision to attend the Fort Sorrel peace meeting.

Much as he hated to leave a promising coon hunt before the hounds sang to the skies that they had run old ringtail up a tree, the Reverend Boardwell did so. In the morning he would be leaving for Fort Sorrel and wished to catch some sleep before doing so.

He saw the two shapes rise from the gate in his home's picket fence, but failed to take alarm. Too late he realized that they were not a couple of his hunting companions returned with news of a success on another part of Hurricane Creek.

"Are you white-eye God-man who come to Comanches?" asked the man at the left.

"I am," Boardwell agreed. "Who are—"

Raw and rank to his nostrils came the smell of rancid antelope grease as the men sprang toward him and he saw steel glinting in their hands. Although he carried a shotgun under his arm, Boardwell never thought to use it; could not in fact, as he had removed the shells on approaching the edge of town. He let the gun fall and launched a punch, feeling his knuckles smash the nose of the man on his right. Bringing his knife across in the sideways stroke, which formed the second blow in the Indian method, the other man sank it deep into Boardwell's side and ripped savagely. Almost the last sound the preacher heard as pain knifed through him was the deep-throated Comanche coup claim.

"*A'he!*" grunted the attacker. "I claim it!"

Ignoring the blood that spurted from his nose, the first man drove down his knife in a savage chop which sank it deep into the reeling preacher's back. Boardwell crumpled forward and collapsed to the ground. With a snarl of rage the injured first attacker dropped to his knees alongside the feebly moving, dying man, tore off and hurled aside the low-crowned black hat, then put his knife to work once again. His companion, more practical—and anyway having counted the first coup—took up the shotgun and rifled Boardwell's pockets for shells to use in it.

On waking and finding her husband had not come to bed, Mrs. Boardwell rose. She crossed to the window, drew back the curtains, looked down—and started screaming. Attracted by the screams, men and women came running. Many of them wished that they had not when they drew near and saw the full horror of the preacher's murder.

"H—he's been scalped!" gasped a man.

"This's Injun work!" another said. "Get up a posse. We'll find the murdering red savages."

A laudable ambition, but one that came to nothing. Although a posse was formed and duly went out, while the telegraph wires sang a warning to every peace officer in the area, no trace of Boardwell's killers could be found. By the time the murder was discovered, the killers had covered thirty miles and rode on as only Comanches could; keeping out of sight even though they passed through a fairly well-populated section of the Lone Star State.

Although Boardwell's killers escaped, word of his death went out and increased the objections of those people opposed to making any kind of peace with the Comanches. It also cost Dusty Fog's party a valuable supporter.

Rance Counter owned a ranch the size of a small eastern county and more cattle than he could guess at. If he signed a draft for ten, or even twenty, thousand dollars, it would be honored in almost any bank or business house in Texas. But when he lost fifteen dollars and fifty cents in the stud poker pot, he swore to regain it no matter how long it took.

While the loss of the money would make no difference to him, Rance Counter strongly objected to it going to his best friend, foreman, and greatest poker rival, Tule Bragg. When playing poker Bragg availed himself of every legal advantage and possessed a number of highly irritating methods of handling his opponents. While dealing he formed the habit at the crucial stage of the game of looking at each card and sniggering knowingly before tossing it to the waiting recipient. Such a tactic, accompanied by comments on his boss's ability as a poker player, so clouded Rance's judgment that he stayed in a pot when every instinct warned him to fold.

"Don't let it worry you, Rance," purred Bragg, dragging in the pot. "You sure came out vice-president."

"Just hand over those damned cards and don't waste time!" Rance growled.

The surrounding cowhands exchanged nudges and grins. Unless they missed their guess, and none of them figured they did, it would be a long, hard night.

Squatting in the darkness two all-but-naked Waw'ai braves tested their knife blades and watched the door into which Rance Counter had entered shortly after night fell. Patient as growing plants the Indians waited for the giant rancher to emerge and return to the ranch house. Hour after hour rolled by, light after light around the building going out until only one remained. Still the rancher did not make his appearance. Shortly before dawn the ranch cook and louse came into view and the Indians withdrew.

Not knowing that the game had saved his life, Rance Counter scooped up a pot that put him on the winning side of the ledger. "There's no point in going to bed now," he drawled, looking through the window at the lightening sky. "May as well have breakfast and get ready to go down into Mexico and pick up that herd of cattle."

"Unless he's my boss I can't stand a hombre who quits a winner," grunted Bragg, estimating that in twelve hours of highly skilled play he had lost the sum of thirty-eight cents.

When going into Mexico to purchase cheap cattle Rance Counter took no chances of being robbed. Accompanied by a bunch of his riders he left the Waw'ai no opportunity to follow the Death Bringer's orders. After two more nights of disappointment they concluded their medicine must be bad and turned back to Texas.

The fates did not smile upon Colonel Hedley Huckfield, Ninth U.S. Cavalry, in such a fortunate manner. Unlike many of his compatriots, probably because his experience of Indian warfare went back farther and he possessed a more accurate picture of *all* its ramifications, Huckfield wanted an acceptable treaty. Leaving his regiment he rode toward Fort Sorrel with the intention of throwing his weight on the side of the men who wished to make the correct type of peace. By doing so he might blast his Army career, but he did not care. Retirement loomed too close for him to worry over such a detail.

Always a light sleeper, and never more so than when camped with only a small escort in possibly hostile country, Huckfield woke at the slight noise made by the man who slipped into his Sibley tent.

"Who's th—!" he began, reaching for the revolver that lay close to his hand and staring at the shape which reared up alongside his cot.

Bringing up the revolver Huckfield became sickeningly conscious that he did not hold his tried and true Army Colt. Instead he gripped a present from his wife; one of the new Smith & Wesson metal cartridge revolvers that had become all the rage back East. A good gun mechanically, accurate and possessing certain advantages over the percussion-fired Army Colt—but only .32 in caliber. Adequate to kill a man, of course, especially at close range; yet lacking the Army Colt's .44 caliber knock-down punch.

Brought out of their sleep by the sound of the shot, Huckfield's escort dashed from their pup tents toward the Colonel's Sibley. They found an Indian, shot in the chest, trying to crawl to the gash he had cut in the Sibley's wall to gain entrance; and Huckfield dead on the cot, knifed through the heart. Unfortunately for Huckfield, and the peace between the white and red races, the Smith & Wesson's .32 bullet had failed to kill or prevent the Waw'ai from delivering a fatal knife-thrust after being hit.

"Damned stinking, lousy Indian!" growled one of the

escort, kicking the grease-covered body savagely. "And the colonel was going to speak up for them being treated right."

Despite the fact that he had never served in any branch of the U.S. or any other, army, or attained greater rank than sergeant as a member of the volunteer Texas Rangers, Charles Goodnight bore the title "Colonel." Texas awarded its favorite sons, when they reached a suitable age, with one of two honorary titles: "Judge" and "Colonel." Only a show of wisdom, not necessarily legal training, entitled a man to the former title. To gain the second he must be a born fighter and a natural leader of men. Charles Goodnight could claim to be both.

All through the Civil War he had roamed the Texas range country, fighting Indians and trying to hold their depredations in check. He knew the Comanche as friend and respected them as enemy. Being aware of the cost in human lives that a sensible treaty could avert, he traveled to Fort Sorrel; intending to throw his not inconsiderable influence on the side of Ole Devil Hardin's representative.

Instinct gained by years of Indian-fighting and riding dangerous trails made Goodnight as wary as a much-hunted Texas red wolf. Throughout the day he had been continually nagged by the thought that somebody was following him. No matter how he watched his back trail, he failed to see any sign of the hostile presence he felt in the vicinity. That meant most likely an Indian was trailing him. Without being egotistical Goodnight doubted if a white man could follow him through such open country and remain unseen.

When night fell, Goodnight halted his horse and dropped quickly from its saddle to flop belly first and lay an ear to the ground. The following men must have real sharp ears, for they also stopped their mounts. Not quite quickly enough, though, and Goodnight heard enough to tell him two men on unshod horses were dogging his tracks. The latter fact pointed with almost absolute certainty to Indians. Which made them just that much more difficult and dangerous to handle.

In appearance Goodnight might have been a typical Comanche by build; except that no Nemenuh ever sported a neatly trimmed full beard. He stood five feet nine, with broad shoulders and a barrel of a chest, which hinted at the powerful, if chunky, body's strength. A costly white, Texas-style Stetson sat on a close-cropped head of grizzled brown hair. What skin showed on his face had the color of old saddle-leather. Sun-squinted brown eyes held a hint of humor, alert in their keenness. Clad in good quality range clothes, instead of the usual calfskin vest he wore one made from the rosette-marked hide of a jaguar that had strayed up out of Old Mexico and made the mistake of allowing itself to cross his rifle sights. That vest had gone through a whole heap of Indian-fighting, being worn so that his enemies could identify him and know that the one they called "Dangerous Man" rode against them. Matched rosewood butted Army Colts rode the two contoured holsters of his gun belt and a Winchester rested in the saddle boot under his left leg. If trouble came, Goodnight reckoned he ought to be able to handle it.

Rising, he swung into his big roan stallion's saddle and started the horse moving at a fast walk. Without a doubt the following pair meant mischief and it would take some smart thinking to avoid becoming their victim.

Silently, but bitterly, Goodnight cursed his decision not to bring his foreman or another member of the ranch crew along. If he had only done so, solving the problem would be simple; slip out of the saddle with rifle in hand, allowing the other man to ride away with both horses and talking as if Goodnight accompanied him. Then when the trailing pair came up, Goodnight could hand them the surprise of their lives.

Unfortunately, being alone, he could not follow the plan. Well trained his horse might be, but not sufficiently so to carry on walking without a rider for the time necessary to allow Goodnight's pursuers to catch up. Some other means must be devised, and until that happened, all the rancher could do was keep moving.

Holding his horse to a steady walk Goodnight remained alert for any opportunity and ready to catch the slightest warning sound. Apparently the following men did not intend to close with him, while he moved, for their horses came no closer. In fact if they had not stopped each time he halted, he might have thought them to be no more than chance travelers.

"Damn it all, hoss," he said to the stallion between his legs. "I don't aim to keep on riding through the night."

Already the basis of an idea began to form. Riding on until he found a hollow that might serve as a camping spot, Goodnight drew rein. On dropping down and placing his ear to the ground, he found that the two men also stopped and estimated them to be almost half a mile behind. Apparently they were sitting their horses, waiting for him to make his next move. So he came to his feet and made it.

Searching the hollow he found sufficient fuel to light a small fire. He moved for a time, as a man would when setting up camp, certain that his pursuers could not see him. Then, taking a silk bandana from his pocket, he stretched out on the ground again. With the bandana spread out he laid his ear upon it. Some quality in silk magnifies sounds transmitted through the ground, and with the bandana's aid Goodnight could form a better idea of the other men's movements. Any lingering doubts as to their intentions died away as he found the men to be advancing cautiously on foot.

Patient as any Indian, although not a little pleased at his shrewd assessment of the situation, Goodnight lay and listened. He figured the men would sneak in on foot rather than chance bringing their horses closer; and based his plan on that fact. Nearer they came, drawing farther away from their horses all the time. In a few seconds they ought to be in sight of his camp. The time had come to act.

Rising swiftly to his feet Goodnight pocketed the bandana and stepped to his waiting horse. Up in the saddle he set the roan running and over its drumming hooves heard the startled exclamations of the men. Beyond the fire's flickering glow he need not fear any but a chance bullet should shots be fired after him. None came and he swung at an angle to his original line. Timing the period it would take his pursuers to run back to their horses and take up the chase, Goodnight slowed the roan and then brought it to a halt in the shelter of a clump of mesquite.

On checking the ground-carried sounds he found no cause for alarm. His two hunters appeared to have fallen for the trick and he heard their horses go by a long way off. As long as he made a dry camp, without a fire, he doubted if they would find him until daylight and then only had they retraced their tracks and taken up his trail.

Dawn came and found Goodnight in his saddle. He traveled, as so often before when scouting for Indians, with caution and exercised all his skill at avoiding being seen. So well had Goodnight learned his work that he out-Indianed the pair of Waw'ai braves sent by the Death Bringer to kill him. By the time they found Goodnight's trail, he had built up such a lead that they could not hope to catch him before he reached the safety of Fort Sorrel.

It might appear strange that the son of one of Texas's best-loved and most respected men—and a noted lawyer in his own right—should be sleeping in the barn of the Rock Fall relay station when Wells Fargo provided reasonable accommodation for its passengers. Yet Temple Houston did so while waiting for the stagecoach to continue its journey to Fort Sorrel.

A man as tall as Mark Counter and almost as broad

across the shoulders, Houston did not slim down so much at the middle, but still gave the impression of great strength. He wore a fringed buckskin jacket over a white, frilly-bosomed shirt and a necktie made from a rattlesnake's hide; Levi's pants hanging cowhand style outside his riding boots. Flaxen hair framed a strong, intelligent face tanned by much outdoor living. Hanging on the wall of the stall close by him were a costly white Stetson hat of Texas fashion, and a good-quality gun belt with an ivory-handled Army Colt in the contoured cross-draw holster at the left side.

While young, Temple Houston had the name for being a shrewd lawyer. He also possessed his father's ability to rub shoulders with all classes of people and win their respect. Like Sam Houston, Temple knew the Comanche and aimed to do all he could to make the treaty signing a success.

Traveling to Fort Sorrel by stagecoach had seemed like a real good idea, especially as he aimed to take along his highly prized Plott hound. Officers on frontier posts eagerly sought diversions to relieve the boredom and were not averse to making bets in hard cash on a variety of things. So Houston brought along a dog speedy enough to run down a fleeing coyote; knowing he stood a good chance of meeting men who refused to believe it possible and willing to lay money on their beliefs.

Unfortunately the coach already held passengers; two U.S. senators on their way to Fort Sorrel and one of the pair's daughter. A remarkably pretty and shapely young woman, she brought to frontier Texas a touch of elegant city life—and a barbered, yapping French poodle complete with a pink bow in its topknot. Any hope Houston might have held of a mild flirtation went out of the window as Lazy, the seventy-five-pound Plott hound,* dem-

* For a description and information about the Plott hound read *Hound Dog Man*.

onstrated a laudable desire to tear the noisy white bundle to ribbons. Miss Cornelia Waterhouse, only daughter of Senator Jubal V. Waterhouse from New Jersey, was not amused.

Relations had become strained during the journey. At the relay station a further party of politicians awaited the stage's arrival and Amelia found that she must share a room with the wives of two Democratic senators who stated their objection to having a Republican's dog in with them. Not wishing to have Lazy in the same building with the poodle, Houston took the Plott into the barn. On hearing the beginning of the interparty wrangling on his return, the Texan decided to join his dog in preference to listening to politicians squabble all night.

Having seen Houston board the stage at his home on the edge of Austin and followed in the hope of finding a chance to carry out the Death Bringer's orders, the two Waw'ai braves waited until after midnight and then slipped silently toward the barn.

Silent they might move to human ears, but the big Plott heard them as he lay close to his sleeping master. Deep and low a growl rumbled in the dog's throat and Houston woke instantly. Seeing the door of the barn start to inch slowly open, he silenced the dog with a gesture and drew his Colt. A lantern glowed over the door, in case anybody arrived during the night and wished to put up a horse. Watching the patch of light Houston saw first one and then the other Indian slide through it.

One glance told Houston all he needed to know, although he put the visit down to a raiding mission on the stabled horses. So it came as something of a surprise when he saw the men, knives in hand, making straight for him. Lazy tugged at the restraining hand on his collar and the Indians saw the movement.

"Kill!" hissed the taller brave and lunged forward.

With a roaring snarl Lazy tore free from Houston's grasp and hurled upward at the Indian. Seventy-five pounds of hard-muscled fighting dog drove at the Waw'ai and took him by surprise. Only just in time did he throw up his arm to defend his throat, and Lazy's jaws gripped it with crushing power. Hurled backward by the big hound's weight, the Waw'ai tripped and crashed to the ground.

Houston's Colt roared, sending a bullet into the head of the second Waw'ai as the Indian started to leap forward in his direction. Knowing what the Waw'ai's state of undress and grease-coated body meant, the big Texan took no chances and shot for an instant kill. Unlike the unfortunate Colonel Huckfield, Houston held a revolver adequate to his needs and rolled aside to avoid a dead Indian falling onto him. Not quite sure how many enemies might be on hand, Houston rose, dived over the side of the stall, and into the welcome shadows beyond. He heard voices raised at the main building and came cautiously to his feet. A change in the sound of the Waw'ai's screams told Houston that Lazy did good work.

Moving forward Houston approached where the dog and Indian struggled on the floor. After paralyzing the man's right arm, Lazy chopped at the left and caused it to be jerked away. Every Plott was a vicious fighter, born with a killer instinct invaluable in a hunting dog. So Lazy drove for the man's throat and powerful jaws sank the long canine teeth home savagely into flesh. Although Houston sprang forward as soon as he knew he could do so without winding up taking yet another Waw'ai's knife in his back, he arrived and dragged Lazy away too late to save the Plott's victim. Blood spurted from a hideous wound in the Waw'ai's throat, pulsing forth in a manner that told of a severed large artery or vein.

"You sure made a mess of him, Lazy," Houston told the Plott as men came running toward the barn. "It's a pity. I'd sure like to have asked him what brings Waw'ais down this way hunting scalps. Know one thing, though. This isn't going to make that pretty li'l eastern gal feel one bit happier to know me, way she talked about Indians."

CHAPTER FIVE

THE DEATH BRINGER'S VISION

Erected close to the Kicking Horse Creek about three miles above where it flowed into the Brazos River, the Waw'ai camp appeared on the surface to be little different from any other Comanche band's village. Some fifty tepees, built on the four-pole foundation and tilted slightly backward in the Nemenuh fashion, formed a rough circle around the dwelling of the chief. Close to each tepee stood tethered the owner's favorite horse so as to be instantly available if needed.

It might have been a normal scene but for the absence of old people. Usually there would have been *tsukup,* old men, supervising Mexican prisoner-apprentices who built saddles, or making bows, shields, and arrows to be sold to brave-heart warriors who had no time to waste producing their own. *Pu'ste,* old women, ought to be instructing the *tuepet* girls approaching adolescence, in those things a female Comanche needed to know, but none appeared to be doing so.

Instead the camp held only *tuivitsi,* young unmarried braves, and grown men still capable of riding the warpath, unmarried maidens and younger wives; brought along to erect tents, repair clothes, and cook food, work beneath the dignity of a Comanche man unless forced by the more dire of circumstances.

All of which would have presented a sinister significance to Billy Salmon, half-breed scout for the U.S. Army, had he been performing his official duties in a loyal manner.

Riding toward the village Salmon read the signs. He also exhibited a complete lack of caution, which either implied great trust in the current peaceful condition existing between the white folks and the majority of Comanches, or some knowledge that ensured his safety.

Engaged in the serious business of sitting before his tepee and waiting the arrival of his next meal, a *tuivitsi* studied the approaching half-breed with cold eyes. Restraining a desire to try out the effect of a recently acquired Spencer carbine on the newcomer, the *tuivitsi* rose and walked to the central tepee. On entering he looked at the man and woman who occupied it.

"The half-breed from the fort is coming," he announced.

"Then let him come," ordered the woman, although her companion was war chief of the village. "We still need him."

Despite the fact that a woman usually stood lower than a good horse, though higher than a pack mule, on the Comanche scale of usefulness, the *tuivitsi* did not argue. People who crossed the Death Bringer rarely lived long enough to boast of doing it.

In her youth the woman known as the Death Bringer had been a mighty pretty Mexican girl. Taller and more slender than the Comanche women, her grace and light feet gave her the name of Fire Dancer among the Pehnane. Only occasionally did the Comanche mistreat children prisoners, preferring to keep them alive and healthy as slaves. Eventually the slaves could become accepted as members of the band and enjoy all the rights of a Comanche by birth.

Certainly Fire Dancer showed no signs of her slave beginnings. Still slender, although her hair had turned gray, she wore a buff-colored buckskin dress with luxuriously fringed sleeves and colorful bead designs and spirit patterns. Beaded moccasins graced her feet, but the warm weather did away with the need for the highly ornamented leggings she wore in the winter. Her face still retained traces of its beauty but bore also a hint of the savage nature underneath.

Although in camp, on an ordinary day Sidewinder wore his ornamented elk-skin shirt, which extended to below the level of his leggings' tops and covered his traditional breechclout. He had rattlesnake skin instead of the usual polecat or other fur fringe on his moccasins. Typical Comanche, he was stocky, medium size, and his war bonnet framed a face that bore the stamp of real cruelty on it. Around his waist hung a gun belt with a Green River knife sheathed at the left and a Freeman Army revolver rode holstered at the right. If he objected to his mother giving orders, he hid his feelings admirably.

While not a man sensitive to atmosphere Salmon never felt entirely easy when in the presence of Sidewinder and the Death Bringer. Yet he knew that his usefulness to them gave him immunity as long as it lasted. When it ended, he would go the way of any other Army scout should he fail to learn the fact in time.

A tall man, Indian-dark with surly features framed by lank black hair, he dressed in a fringed buckskin shirt, cavalry campaign hat and trousers, and knee-long moccasins. He did not fail to notice the avaricious way in which Sidewinder eyed the Army Colt holstered cavalry-fashion on his belt and wondered how long it would be before the chief decided to take possession of it.

"Well?" demanded Fire Dancer.

"It's been a long, hard ride," Salmon hinted.

"I'll have food brought to you," she promised. "What is the news from the fort?"

"Have any of *the* ones come for the council?" Sidewinder asked.

"Goodnight is there," Salmon told him uneasily. "Also Houston's son."

"I never thought we would have success on all of them," commented Fire Dancer philosophically.

"Diablo Viejo could not come," Salmon went on, and continued before he raised false hopes, "but he sent the one called Magic Hands to speak for him. Also the son of 'Big' Counter came."

An almost animal-sounding snarl left Sidewinder's lips and his mother hissed, "These stupid Waw'ai dogs. If only they were Kweharehnuh or Pehnane—"

"The God-man died and so did Colonel Huckfield," Salmon put in, feeling that he had better give his host and hostess *some* good news.

Both Fire Dancer and her son were aware that one name, the one that interested them both, had not been mentioned.

"And what of Cuchilo?" snarled the chief, his hand going in an involuntary move to touch his injured leg.

Sucking in a deep breath Salmon avoided his questioner's eyes and paused as long as he dared before giving an answer he knew would be even more unpopular than the previous news.

"Cuchilo lives."

"So he still lives!" Fire Dancer shouted in a voice throbbing with hate. "And he the one I wanted most to die!"

An even greater uneasiness crept over Salmon as he listened to the woman and wondered at her response to the news that the Ysabel Kid had not been murdered. He put the reaction down to Fire Dancer realizing the Kid's influence on the thinking of the tribal leaders; little knowing that the hatred went much farther back than the organization of the treaty council.

For a prisoner Fire Dancer had done well. She became adopted into the Pehnane and married, as fourth wife, a name-warrior called Bitter Root. Defying convention she worked herself into the position of *pairaivo*, easing the original first wife from their husband's favor. Everything had been going in keeping with Fire Dancer's ideas of the fitness of life when her husband provoked a fatal quarrel with Sam Ysabel.

After that Fire Dancer's numerous sins bounced rapidly back onto her head. The other wives moved fast, repaying her for slights and indignities heaped on them by the young *pairaivo*. Having fathers and brothers to back their claims, the three wives saw that the division of their departed husband's property satisfied them. From being the rich, spoiled *pairaivo* Fire Dancer found herself turned into a widow dependent on the charity of the tribe. She blamed her misfortune on Sam Ysabel, although he did not start the fatal fight, and swore revenge against the white man.

With the Latin's capacity for hate and retaining grudges, she bided her time. Leaving the Pehnane, Fire Dancer traveled to the Kweharehnuh, Antelope, band of the Comanche and settled among them. Four times she married and each husband met a mysterious death after raising her to *pairaivo* and willing her the bulk of his property. Fire Dancer befriended the Kweharehnuh witchwoman to such a degree that she learned many dark and sinister secrets. At last she felt the time had come to return to the Pehnane and extract vengeance on Bitter Root's killer. She failed to achieve anything against Ysabel or his son. In fact her final effort cost several lives and the crippling of her son without bringing about her desire.

Fleeing from the vengeance that she expected to come, Fire Dancer brought her son at last to the Waw'ai band. A storm washed out their tracks and the Civil War of the white men further prevented Sam or Loncey Ysabel hunting her down. Among the Waw'ai, Fire Dancer gained a reputation as medicine woman and witch while her son developed into first a warrior, then war chief due to her driving will.

With the passing of time Fire Dancer's hatred of the Ysabels grew and was transferred to the Pehnane, then the whole of the Comanche nation. Always she sought for a way in which she might bring ruin to the people who gave her a home and at least as good a life as she might have had in the small Mexican village from which a raiding party snatched her. So when the word went out that the old-man chiefs of the major Nemenuh bands aimed to make peace, she thought her vengeance might come to nothing.

The peace council had not been arranged in a matter of days, but worked for and developed over a period of almost two years. Attending talks in her capacity of Waw'ai medicine woman, certain facts became obvious even during the earliest meetings between Comanche and white negotiators. Realizing that peace did not meet with the approval of all white men, including some of those supposedly trying to make it, Fire Dancer turned her natural bent for intrigue and witchwoman knowledge to good account. She found the right men and made her proposals. In return for certain concessions, which interested her less than the ultimate effect of her actions on the Comanche people—but proved necessary to lull the white men's suspicions of her motives—Fire Dancer promised to keep alive the bad feeling that existed between many of both peoples.

Using Salmon as a go-between Fire Dancer and her white coplanners exchanged ideas. All the time, while most Comanche bands kept the peace, Sidewinder led his Waw'ai braves on raids of the most vicious kind and fed fuel to the flames a very vocal section of the white nation fanned against negotiations with the Nemenuh.

Despite that, the peace council was arranged. So, too, were plans for wrecking it. With the help of her white allies Fire Dancer sent men out to kill a number of influential friends of the Comanche. From what Salmon had just told her, the plan only partially succeeded and the one person she hoped to be dead more than any of the others still remained alive.

"What other word do you bring from the fort?" she asked after what had been a disturbingly long silence for Salmon.

"The white soldier lance carriers have been sent to bring in the Waw'ai to Fort Sorrel," he answered.

"These I have seen," Fire Dancer commented in a flat voice. "How many of them come?"

"Almost a hundred."

"And what are they to do?"

"Make your people come in. Use force if they have to."

Which meant, as Salmon and Fire Dancer well knew, a fight. Any Comanche still away from the council meeting did not intend to attend and would only be taken there by force. A frown creased Fire Dancer's brow and Salmon's uneasiness leapt even higher as he wondered how she was taking his last piece of news.

"Sit down," she ordered. "I will have food for you. Then I must make medicine. Have no fear, friend, you only brought the news."

Salmon gulped at something that seemed to be blocking his throat. Knowing better than to argue, he sat on his heels and watched Fire Dancer leave the tepee. Sidewinder did not follow his mother, but hunkered down facing the scout and watched Salmon with cold, unwinking eyes. That did nothing to improve Salmon's appetite, already made jumpy by the knowledge that Fire Dancer used poison as a means of disposing of people who crossed her. However, the scout managed to force a meal of the inevitable stew down and felt no ill-effects from it. With the meal over he sat faced by the silent chief and waited for Fire Dancer's return. At last the door flap lifted and Fire Dancer entered.

"You can find the lance carriers?" she asked without preamble.

"I reckon I can," agreed Salmon. "They're coming down Elk Creek toward Lovatt City. You'll want me to find them and lead them away from your camp?"

"No. I want you to find them and bring them here."

"Here?" yelped Salmon, and Sidewinder let out a low hiss of breath.

"Toward this camp," confirmed the woman. "But bring them through Wide Valley when you come."

"I can do that," Salmon said. "But how about me?"

"What do you mean?"

"It figures that you're going to fight them soldiers, so where do I come off? I'll be with the soldiers, and your braves don't look too careful at who they're counting coup on when they're in a fight."

"A wise man would make sure that his horse became lame at the right moment," purred Fire Dancer. "All I ask is that you bring the lance carriers into Wide Valley for me."

"That'll be easy. I know their leader and he'll listen to me. By noon in two days' time I'll have them coming into Wide Valley."

Not until after the scout's departure did Sidewinder raise the points that troubled him. Sitting in the tepee he looked at his mother.

"Aiee! These Waw'ai will not have stomach when they see they face lance carriers."

"White-eye lance carriers," corrected Fire Dancer. "When I was a child in Mexico, I saw lance carriers and know how they fight. Go and have the camp cried that there will be a war dance this night, and when you return I will tell you how you will defeat the lance carriers and what you must do after they are beaten."

No Comanche would think of going upon a warpath without celebrating the occasion with a dance, and this itself called for a special ceremony. After receiving his instructions from Fire Dancer, Sidewinder made a start.

Normally the organizer of a war party called in his friends, or other name-warriors, to discuss the proposed raid; but Sidewinder had such a reputation among the Waw'ai that he felt he could dispense with formalities. Nor did time permit an extended period of preparation, with racks of lances supporting shields gathering medicine strength from the sun before the organizer's tepee and women going about to induce recruitment by persuading men to join the party. The latter did not prove necessary, as no man in that village dared refuse the Death Bringer's wishes.

The traditional parade of warriors could not be overlooked. About sundown Sidewinder led his party in single file and paraded four times through the village. Each man wore his medicine paint and war clothes, carrying his arms to show his readiness to make war. Among the party three men each carried a *naivi,* maiden, dressed in male's clothing on their horses, seated behind them. This signified that the man in question had performed the honored feat of carrying a wounded or unhorsed companion out of a fight, or collected a dead brave to prevent the body falling into enemy hands and bring bad luck down on the war party.

When night came, the entire population of the village gathered about the large fire in the center of the tepee circle. Forming a rough circle they left an opening in their ranks facing the distant Wide Valley, as required by tradition. Not all the braves would be going, it being necessary to leave a small force to guard the village. Only those actually riding with Sidewinder could dance, and each had a woman to partner him.

Accompanied by drums and the singing of those who did not dance, warriors and their partners performed the long-established steps of the ceremony. At intervals various members of the party halted the dancing to recount their best coup, telling it to rouse the spirits of the younger members and show what kind of company could be expected in the dangerous times ahead. Now and then a warrior and *naivi* slipped off into the darkness; no maiden would think of refusing to accompany a man who could bring back much loot, and would be grateful for services rendered, or might die in battle and so deserved comfort.

Through the night, warriors danced, or sat singing. They sang war chants, but also raised their voices in love songs. Then an expectant silence fell over the crowd and Sidewinder rose from his place of honor. The time had come for the party's war leader to address them.

Standing in the circle's center, his face made even more evil by the flickering glow of the fire's flames, Sidewinder warned of the coming of the white soldiers. He told how his party must go out to battle and destroy the hated intruders and then promised that, on achieving victory, they would make a raid to bring in much loot and provide unlimited opportunities to count coup. With skilled oratory he called upon his companions to display their usual courage, explaining that a resounding victory would make them the supreme Nemenuh tribe. It would also bring flocking to them all the warriors of the other bands who wanted no such foolishness as peace with the white invaders of Comancheria. At the head of an ever-growing army the Waw'ai under Sidewinder would sweep the hated white man to wherever they had come from and bring back the good old days once more.

"We must defeat the lance carriers first, though," he warned his men. "But I have medicine for that."

"The Death Bringer's medicine?" asked one of the braves.

"My medicine," agreed Fire Dancer. "I have seen that you will defeat the white lance carriers, then sweep across the prairie to greater victories. For who will dare stand in the way of brave-hearts who have defeated the carriers of lances?"

Knowing in what respect they themselves held warriors brave enough to carry a lance into battle, none of the listening crowd could doubt that Fire Dancer's predictions would bring about the desired result. Even those who did not relish tangling with lance carriers, even white ones, began to take faith when they heard that the full, malignant medicine *puha* of the Death Bringer backed them.

Fortunately none of the party thought to ask about the men sent out to kill and so far not returned, or knew of the various failures, or they might have felt less faith in their witchwoman's powers.

CHAPTER SIX

A RESPONSIBLE CHORE FOR CAPTAIN FOG

"It's a sight to see," commented Dusty Fog as, accompanied by his friends, he rode his seventeen-hand paint stallion—the one that had crippled Ole Devil—on the final stage of the journey to Fort Sorrel.

"I never afore saw so many Comanche together," agreed Mark Counter, studying the clusters of tepees that formed a half-circle beyond the log-walled perimeter of the fort. "Those Yankee soldiers'll be sweating all ways."

"What'd you expect?" demanded the Kid. "Us Nemenuh aren't real smart like you white folks, but we know a whole heap better than let just the old-man chiefs come in to make a treaty. This way we stand a better-than-even chance of getting the chiefs back again."

"Don't you-all trust us white folks, then?" grinned Mark, sitting easily afork his huge blood-bay stud horse; a light rider who took less out of his mount than a less skilled man of smaller size.

Allowing his magnificent white stallion to fall behind his companions, the Kid moved it closer to Mark. Before the white came within range, Mark hurriedly removed his leg from the stirrup and clear of the big stallion's shapely head. With the air of one who had proved his point the Kid resumed his position level with the others.

"We trust you white folks as much as you trust this old hoss of mine," he assured Mark.

One member of the party, apart from the Kid, regarded

the sight of the tepees with pleasure. Driving a buggy, with two pack horses fastened to its rear, Professor Hollenheimer studied the groups of Indian dwellings with eager attention. He ignored the view of the fort, having seen many of them during his visits to different Indian tribes. While the materials used for construction differed to suit local conditions, the position of the various buildings altered, the basic layout remained the same. Guardhouse and cells by the main entrance, officers' country made neat and homey, the Spartan simplicity of the barrack blocks. Stables, picket lines, stores and administration sections, the saddlers' and farriers' departments spaced around the parade square, which in turn had a lane of jumps for the horses on two of its sides. None of that particularly interested Hollenheimer. His eyes feasted on the potential source of learning offered by the assembled Comanches.

"Can you tell me what bands are here?" he asked, looking at the Kid.

"That bunch at the far side are Tanima, Liver Eaters," the Kid replied and his finger moved to the next loose circle of tents. "You can always tell the Detsanawyehka, they're real slovenly in setting up camps. Their name means Wanderers-Who-Make-Bad-Camps. The Yamparikuh, Yap Eaters, are next to the wanderers. Then there's the Iteha'c. They always put up more pemmican than they can eat and throw away all that's not eaten comes spring, so old folks used to find the meat all black and spoiled and start calling them the Burnt Meat band."

"How about that small group by the stream?" asked Hollenheimer excitedly.

"Pahuraix, Water Horse band."

"Is that the same as the Par-Kee-Na-Um?"

"Sure, Professor. It means Water People. They always make camp on the bank of a lake or river. Coming by them, that next group, there's a sight."

"What are they?"

"Kweharehnuh," breathed the Kid. "The Antelope band. Happen they come in, the treaty's safe."

"Is it?" said Hollenheimer.

"Sure. The Kweharehnuh are as tough as they come and none too friendly with the whites. If anybody stays out, it'll be them."

"Who are the big group of tepees separated from the others?"

"My people," said the Kid, a note of pride in his voice. "The Pehnane."

"Then all the bands are here," Hollenheimer remarked.

"Not all of them, Professor," Dusty corrected. "Lon never mentioned the Waw'ai."

Until the attempted murders at the OD Connected, Dusty had barely heard of the Waw'ai band. Since then his interest in that particular section of the Comanche nation grew and he looked forward to meeting the Waw'ai elders.

"Most likely any of them who're here have bedded down with the Pahuraix," guessed the Kid. "That way they can listen in on what's said and take word back to the war chiefs. I reckon I'll go take Grandpappy Long Walker his presents, Dusty."

"Sure," agreed Dusty. "I'd like to come around and meet him again later in the day."

"Feel free," the Kid offered. "You'll be safe enough in any of the camps and nowhere safer than among the Pehnane."

Unfastening the halter rope of one of the pack horses, the Kid gave a cheery grin to his friends and rode away from them. The horse carried presents and the butchered carcass of a white-tailed deer that he'd killed on the trip. While passing among the Pehnane tepees he called greetings and received salutations from a number of people. After the war ended, he had found time to visit his grandfather and found himself still remembered.

A heavily built old woman wearing spotlessly clean buckskin dress and the ornaments of one well endowed with wealth looked up as the Kid drew rein alongside her. Grave of feature, her age-wrinkled face creased in a smile while her lively eyes studied him.

"Greetings, *pia*," the Kid said, using the respectful term for aunt. "I bring meat for your fire."

"I thank you, Cuchilo," replied Raccoon Talker, senior medicine woman of the Pehnane and who had acted as midwife at his birth.

"And what do you see ahead, old one?" asked the Kid, after dismounting and unloading a quarter of the deer's carcass from the pack horse.

"Trouble comes, Cuchilo. This council will not go easily. There are men, white and Nemenuh, who do not want peace."

The Kid listened attentively, having seen something of the old woman's predictions coming true. Back when he rode on his first buffalo hunt she warned him of danger and his horse fell—or had it been shot? He still did not know for sure—while running a bull. Later, while the Kid camped over a mile from the village so as to train his newly acquired white stallion, Raccoon Talker told his two best friends that he was in danger, needing their help; which he did. Accompanied by a group of captive boys Fire Dancer and No Father tried to murder the Kid and steal the horse. A twinge of regret ran through the Kid as he remembered that both his friends died in the fighting.

"They died as men, Cuchilo," Raccoon Talker remarked. "It was a good way to die."

If the Kid felt any surprise at the way she followed his thoughts, he hid them and nodded in agreement. Any Nemenuh who met his end in battle, especially while trying to help a friend, could be assured of a place in the Land of Good Hunting.

"What of No Father, *pia?*" he asked. "I hear that one is a great man now."

"A gopher is a great one—to worms," the old woman answered dryly.

"Is he here?"

"Neither he nor that blackhearted witch who spawned him."

"Now, that's a *real* pity," said the Kid mildly, and in English.

"This is a peace council, Cuchilo," Raccoon Talker warned, although to the best of his knowledge she spoke none of the English language. "You could not satisfy your revenge oath here."

"You could be right at that," grinned the Kid. "I must see my grandfather."

"And I must cook my meat," smiled Raccoon Talker; then she nodded to where a bunch of young braves played *tir' awwawkaw,* throwing specially designed arrows by hand at a mark. "The *tuivitsi* are restless."

"*Tuivisti* always are," drawled the Kid tolerantly, having ridden sufficient war trails, despite his youth, to be classed as *tehnap,* a seasoned warrior.

Like a cowhand, no Comanche brave walked when he could ride, so the Kid swung back into his saddle and continued to ride. He stopped off to leave another present of meat with the family of Wepitapu'ni, War Club, who acted as his foster parents after his mother's death. War Club was over at the Iteha'c camp playing the old Comanche gambling game of "hands," so the Kid promised to return and rode onto his grandfather's group of tepees.

Admiration glowed in his grandmother's eyes as he dismounted. Greeting the old woman warmly, the Kid distributed presents and then walked over to the main tepee, having learned he would find Long Walker there. Halting outside the door, a grin came to the Kid's lips.

"*Ehhaitsma,*" he called, using the answer given when the grandfather visited a birth tepee to inquire as to the

sex of the new baby and meaning "It's your close friend."
With the father away on the warpath or other man's business, most of the baby boy's upbringing and training fell on the maternal grandfather, and he did indeed become the child's close friend.

Lifting the flap the Kid entered the tepee. Long Walker advanced with a welcoming smile. Medium-sized, with a stocky, iron-hard frame that advancing years had not weakened, and a strong, dignified face framed by whitening hair, Long Walker looked much as when the Kid saw him last. He wore the ordinary buckskin clothing of a wealthy Comanche during normal times. In the center of the tepee stood a rawhide wardrobe case, shaped like a white man's letter envelope and called a *nat'sakena,* which held his best clothing, and a *tunawaws* tube-shaped bag containing his warbonnet, war paint, brush and mirror. When the time came for the big council, Long Walker could appear dressed as befitting the senior war leader of the Pehnane band.

"Greetings, *tawk,*" said the Kid, using the word by which grandfather and grandson addressed each other.

"It is good to see you, *tawk,*" replied Long Walker, shaking hands white-man fashion. "Is Magic Hands with you?"

"He went into the fort to see the chief of the soldiers."

"It is as it should be."

"How goes it with you, *tawk?*" asked the Kid.

"Well enough. Some of the *tuivitsi* grow restless and talk of going back to the old ways. It is only the old ones who know there can be no going back."

"One of the old ones must have told you, *tawk,*" the Kid said. "It will be many summers before Long Walker is *tsukup.*"

"Living among the white men has not made you forget how to talk to your elders," smiled the chief.

"I am still a Pehnane," answered the Kid. "Now I have presents and then we eat."

At the main gate to the fort a sentry halted Dusty's party and the sergeant of the guard came over. Being a grizzled veteran who knew all sides of Indian wars, he showed some relief at hearing the identity of the new arrivals.

"You'll be housed in officer's country, gents," he said. "Here's the officer of the day. Likely he'll show you where to go."

"Now, there's something I've not seen in a long time, Dusty," Mark put in.

Following the direction of his amigo's gaze Dusty saw a couple of soldiers riding by and understood the comment. They wore the usual blue kepi and uniform of the U.S. Army with the cavalry's yellow stripe down the trousers' legs, sat a normal McClellan saddle, and might have been the guidon carriers for their company. Only, no guidon rode on a nine-foot shaft of best Norway fir, or carried an eleven-inch-long, needle-pointed steel tip.

"Lancers," Dusty said and looked at the sergeant. "I thought you gave them up in the war."

"And so we did," the noncom agreed, eyeing the Lancers with faint contempt. "But some foreign duke came over here and got up a company of 'em at his own expense. Look real fancy, Cap'n Fog, don't they."

"*Real* fancy," agreed Dusty, recalling the Kid's comments on the nature of a Comanche warrior who carried a lance into battle.

Before he could say more, Dusty saw the smartly dressed officer of the day draw near. Studying the uniform and general appearance of the lieutenant, Dusty pegged him as a well-to-do career officer. Handsome, tall, with a cavalryman's carriage, First Lieutenant Farley Manners struck Dusty as being the kind of officer who would go far; and Dusty had something of a way at picking such men. The guard sergeant drew back and Manners introduced himself, eyeing the Texans quizzically.

"General Handiman would like to see you, Captain Fog," the lieutenant told Mark.

"I'll come as soon as I've seen to my horse," Dusty answered, and saw Manners struggle to hold down surprise.

"You are *Captain* Fog?" Manners asked, poker faced by an effort of will.

"So I've been told, mister."

Something in Dusty's tone gave Manners a warning. One did not attain first lieutenant's rank in peacetime without learning the value of discretion and diplomacy. When Manners came to look harder at Dusty, he recognized the real man under the insignificant exterior and figured it would go hard on anybody who crossed the small Texan. Yes, sir; there sat a man who could be *the* Captain Dustine Edward Marsden Fog whose name had been spoken of in rage, mingled with respect and envy, during the war.

"The general said after you'd attended to your horse," Manners agreed, holding back his inclination to stiffen into a brace under the cold gray eyes. It annoyed him to have somebody make him feel like a West Point plebe addressing a *very* senior cadet. "I'll escort you to the stables."

"Who else's here, mister?" Dusty asked as they made their way to the stables.

"Only Colonel Goodnight so far," Manners answered, striding out at a brisk pace. "The senatorial committee are coming in on the evening stage—if they managed to catch it in the first place."

Having served in the Army, if on the other side, and under senior officers of irascible temperament, Dusty and Mark could sympathize with Manners's desire to carry out his orders. So they wasted no time in talk. On arrival at the stables the two Texans put up their horses while an enlisted man saw to the buggy and pack animals. Finding that he had not been invited to meet the general at that point, Hollenheimer promised to see to Dusty and Mark's belongings and attend to settling it in the room allocated to them.

Manners showed some relief as he led the Texans toward a small cabin mostly used as a store for officers' traveling trunks and boxes that would be too large to keep in their limited accommodation. Wishing privacy Handiman had had the cabin turned into a temporary office. After knocking and announcing the two Texans, Manners withdrew.

Big, bluff, capable looking, hard as a combat soldier despite being based in Washington, General Handiman appeared little changed since their last meeting. He had discarded his jacket and wore a dark blue uniform shirt with a wide falling collar and the two stars of a major general on his shoulders. Holding out his hand he walked toward the Texans.

"Dustine, Counter," he greeted. "Do you know Colonel Goodnight?"

"You might say that." Dusty smiled. "Howdy, Uncle Charlie."

"Howdy, Dustine, Mark," Goodnight answered. "Ole Devil all right?"

"Why, sure. Said to me to tell you two not to get too drunk as he can't be here to keep you under control."

"Did you have any trouble getting here, Dusty?" Handiman inquired, face losing its smile.

"Nope," replied Dusty, darting a glance at Goodnight, then to a couple of telegraph message forms that formed the only items on Handiman's desk. "We had a mite at the ranch before we left, though."

"Indian trouble?" asked Handiman.

"You might say that. Three Waw'ais tried to jump Lon and Uncle Devil. Have *you* been having trouble, Uncle Charlie?"

"Not trouble, but close to it," Goodnight replied, and

explained about the men following him. "I can't say as it was Indians, mind."

"We know that a Waw'ai Comanche killed Colonel Huckfield," Handiman put in, nodding to the telegraph forms. "And it's likely that the Reverend Boardwell was murdered by an Indian."

"Have you heard anything from the Big Bend?" Mark asked anxiously.

"Not a word," the general replied.

A small sigh of relief left Mark's lips. If there had been an attempt on his father's life, he could rely upon it that either his brothers or Tule Bragg would send him news of the incident.

"Nothing from Temple Houston?" Dusty asked.

"Not yet."

The situation ran parallel to Mark's case. Unless Houston had been ambushed and killed somewhere that his body could not be found, word was sure to have come in of his death.

"I sure hope old Temple makes it," Mark drawled.

"And so do I," Handiman agreed fervently. "This situation's tense enough without any further complications."

"How do you mean?" Dusty inquired.

"As you know, there've been a heap of objections to the treaty. We've offered the Comanche a fair piece of real good land for their reservation and that doesn't sit right in some places. Word has it that there's a plan to bust the council up and stop the treaty being signed."

"Is that why *you've* been sent?" Mark wanted to know.

"I'm here in my capacity as head of the adjutant general's department," Handiman answered a shade stiffly.

While Goodnight regarded Handiman as a distinguished combat soldier currently acting as a figurehead commander of the U.S. Army's legal department, Dusty and Mark knew that he had been running the Secret Service since Pinkerton's retirement at the end of the war. Clearly Handiman wished to avoid word of his appointment leaking even to Goodnight, and the Texans respected his desire.

"There's smart brains behind the attempts and killings," Dusty said.

"How do you mean?" asked Goodnight.

"Take the way they picked their victims, Uncle Charlie. Every one of them a well-known and well-liked figure who's sympathetic to the Comanche cause. If you'd all been killed, there's precious few would stand up for the Indians. Most of your supporters and all the fence-sitters would allow there's no sense in standing by folks ungrateful enough to murder their friends. And the men behind the attempts likely have the means to get the stories going."

"You mean that white men planned them and used Indians to do the work?"

"That's just what I mean, General," agreed Dusty. "I know that a Comanche can find his way across the range easy enough. But not to go to a town and pick out the right man. We took a prisoner and he told us plenty. A half-breed brought his bunch to the Rio Hondo and they'd laid up a ways off for two days watching for a chance to get Lon and Uncle Devil. Indians alone wouldn't do that."

"Did you find the half-breed?" asked Handiman.

"He lit out when the shooting started. Lon took his trail, but lost it and we hadn't time enough to spend on a long hunt."

"I'm inclined to agree with you, Dustine," Handiman stated. "It goes along with a few things I've learned."

"What I don't get," Goodnight drawled when Handiman did not disclose the nature of his learnings, "is how the Waw'ai come to be mixed in this. They've never been friendly to the whites."

"From what we learned, their witchwoman must be," Mark answered. "She sent the men out to kill and threatened them with a death curse if they failed or talked happen they were caught."

"Then how'd you make him talk?" Goodnight said, knowing something of the store Comanches set by their oaths and curses.

"We played a couple of tricks on him," Dusty replied. "What did you want to see me about, General?"

"This business. What do you suggest we do?"

"How do you mean?"

"Shall we cancel the council until we've made a try at getting the men behind the trouble?"

"If you cancel it now, there won't be one," warned Goodnight. "The Comanche will think this's another trick and pull out."

"I'd say keep it going," Dusty went on. "Only, watch every move. Those jaspers'll try to break it up and we have to stop them. If it fetches them out into the open, we might nail their hides to the wall."

"That's what I thought you'd say," Handiman said. "All right, Dustine. We'll go on with it and I'm relying on you to see that nothing happens. Do what you like. Make any arrangements you want. I'll back you all the way."

"And the Army?"

"You tell me what you want and I'll see you get it," promised Handiman.

"I'll do just that," Dusty drawled. "If there's nothing more right now, sir, I'd like to see Long Walker and ask his opinion on those Waw'ai attacks."

CHAPTER SEVEN

CAPTAIN FOG KEEPS THE PEACE

While General Handiman would have liked to continue the discussion, two things prevented him from doing so. First, he knew that Long Walker expected a courtesy call from Dusty and would cooperate better if he received it. Secondly, the officer of the day sent word that the expected stagecoach had made a record trip and was in sight. Knowing that he must pander to the important passengers' ego, Handiman told Dusty they would meet later and rose to leave. One of the Democratic senators being a family friend, Mark decided to go with Handiman. Goodnight wished to settle in at the officers' quarters. So Dusty walked alone to the Pehnane camp.

A number of troublesome thoughts nagged at Dusty as he approached the tepees. So far everything seemed peaceable enough, the Indians going about their ordinary affairs and ignoring the white folks. However, if some trader started peddling whiskey, or a brave indulged in the ancient Comanche art of horse stealing—to name but two eventualities—the whole situation could blow up. There were enough Comanche braves in the vicinity to start a fair-sized war and likely more within a day's ride just waiting to see what happened.

Having grown tired of their game of *tir'awwawkaw,* the group of *tuivitsi* hung about bored and looking for some diversion. One of them gave his nearest companion a nudge, then nodded to where Dusty approached.

While most Texas ride-plenties were big, dangerous-looking men, this one did not appear to be. It might be amusing to make some sport at the newcomer's expense. With that thought in mind the *tuivitsi* raised his right arm and flicked the throwing arrow in Dusty's direction.

At the door of his tepee Long Walker saw the incident and started to move forward so as to intervene on his visitor's behalf. At his grandfather's side the Kid held out a restraining hand and grinned.

"Leave them, *tawk,*" the Kid advised. "Ole Dusty won't hurt any of them."

While it had not been his young braves' welfare that worried the chief, he halted and watched.

Dusty came to a halt as the throwing arrow sank its point into the ground at his feet. Coming abruptly from his reverie he looked at the bunch of *tuivitsi* and knew exactly what he faced. Often he had seen cowhands or soldiers of that same young age act in such a manner and had the answer to their behavior.

Ignoring the braves as they drew closer Dusty plucked the arrow from the ground. Slowly he lifted it and looked straight at the *tuivitsi*. With a contemptuous gesture Dusty snapped the arrow and flung it aside. A low growl of anger left the lips of the arrow's owner. He had spent much time and effort in producing the arrow; selecting a straight shaft, picking and fitting the feathers, and working to attain a good balance. While he might have taken the destruction had it been done by a Comanche name-warrior, he refused to do so at the hands of a small Texas ride-plenty. Just an instant too late the *tuivitsi* discovered that what he faced was not a small, insignificant cowhand, but a *big,* dangerous grown man.

From hurling away the arrow Dusty's right hand swung across and up. Caught by the full force of a backhand slap the *tuivitsi* went sprawling into his companions' arms and prevented all but one from making any sudden moves. To the side of the rest the unentangled brave started to draw the knife from its sheath at his belt. He learned then how Dusty Fog had gained the name of Magic Hands.

Dusty's left hand flickered across toward his right side in a move so fast that the eye could barely follow it. Out came the left-side Colt, its trigger depressed and hammer drawn back the instant the barrel slanted away from Dusty's body. Shock and astonishment showed on the *tuivitsi's* face and he froze as would any sensible white man when faced with Dusty's lined, cocked, and ready Army Colt. Nor did the rest of the group make any moves. All stood staring as if they could not believe their eyes. So might a diamondback rattlesnake have looked if the rabbit it attacked suddenly proved to have fangs, claws, and a complete immunity to poison.

"The choice is yours," Dusty announced in Spanish, having heard the Kid claim that most Pehnane understood that language.

"Think well, Rides Backward," called Long Walker. "That is Magic Hands."

Slowly the *tuivitsi's* hand came away from the hilt of his knife and his companions lost their hostile intentions fast. No man need feel shame at being beaten by a name-warrior of Magic Hands's standing. Respect flickered on the braves' faces; much the same kind of expression that came to white men of their age on becoming acquainted with Dusty Fog.

"My apologies, Magic Hands," said Long Walker in Spanish, advancing and holding out his hand. "They are only young."

The Colt pinwheeled on Dusty's trigger finger and flipped back into its holster, watched by the young braves, who had never seen a real top gunfighter in action. He looked at the *tuivitsi* with the tolerant acceptance of one who was *tehnap* and could excuse wildness in youth.

"They'll learn," he replied. "Happen they don't do something else foolish and get killed."

"You think like a Comanche," smiled the chief. "Come into my tepee, we have much to say."

On entering the tepee, Dusty settled down to squat on his heels with almost the same ease as his host and the Kid.

"How about the young buck I knocked down, Lon?" he asked.

"He's learned his lesson," drawled the Kid. "A *tuivitsi* who acts up with a *tehnap* asks for all he gets."

"That is so among your people too," smiled Long Walker. "Cuchilo has told me of the Waw'ai, Magic Hands. They tried to kill your uncle."

"And other people," Dusty answered, going on to tell the chief all he learned of the Waw'ai attempts and successes.

"We will go and speak with the Waw'ai old ones," Long Walker declared.

"Will they tell you anything if Fire Dancer put a death curse on them?"

"Fire Dancer never learned how to put on a curse that Raccoon Talker couldn't take off one handed, left handed at that, Dusty," replied the Kid. "You tell Grandpappy what you want to know and he'll see that you get the answers."

"I'd say that the first thing is to learn where the main Waw'ai camp is," Dusty suggested.

"That can be arranged easily," Long Walker promised. "Come, we will see the Waw'ai now. Tonight, Magic Hands, I would ask you to make speech to the chiefs."

"Will they listen to me?"

"They listened when you spoke at the Council of the Devil Gun."

"Then I'll do it," Dusty said.

Leaving the tepee Long Walker told one of his wives to fetch a horse for Dusty. With the party mounted they rode through the village and Dusty learned all he could of the prevailing state of affairs. So far there had been little contact between the assembled Comanches and the white people. Wisely the commanding officer at the fort ruled that the Indian villages be off limits to members of his command. Wishing to avoid any chance of trouble the chiefs ordered their braves to keep out of the fort.

Dusty realized that the placid condition meant little. If there should be an organized plan to disrupt the council, its originators would probably be waiting until the full senatorial committee assembled before starting whatever they had in mind. By proving to such an influential body that the Comanche did not want peace, further attempts at resettling the Indians on decent land would be rigorously opposed at government level.

Yells and whoops came to the trio's ears as they rode toward the Water Horse village and caused them to swing away from their path. Reaching the top of the slope they looked down at the start of a horse race being watched by half-a-dozen soldiers and the same number of Indians.

Only two horses competed in the race, and on the face of it, there hardly seemed any doubt as to the outcome. A small soldier, showing signs of having trained on race-courses back East, rode a big, fine-looking bay; being matched against a big, bulky Comanche afork just about the most ugly and unlikely animal Dusty had seen. Small, Roman-nosed, with a tail that would have looked good on a rat, the Indian pony ought to have been left standing, especially when bearing such a hefty load. Incredibly it was not. Instead the little horse began to draw ahead of its finely built opponent.

"Man, oh, man!" drawled the Kid. "I always knew soldiers weren't smart, but don't this beat all?"

"How do you mean?" asked Dusty, staring at the speeding horses.

"They'd fall for the shell-and-pea game, was it tried on them," the Kid said caustically.

The yells of the soldiers died uncertainly away as they became aware that their horse stood no chance. Racing along at a speed that amazed its white audience, the Indian pony increased its lead to such a point that its rider drew rein and waited for the other horse to draw near, then galloped away again.

Watching the race, if race it could be called, Dusty felt puzzled. Skilled in equestrian matters he could see that the bay was not being held back by its rider; which had at first struck him as a distinct possibility. Knowing soldiers Dusty doubted that they raced for pleasure and had most probably laid bets on their horse winning. They could have planned to let the Indian win by a short lead so as to gain an increase in the bets on a second race. From their reactions Dusty concluded that, if such had been the plan, it went sadly wrong.

"If I wasn't seeing it," Dusty said, starting down toward the audience, "I wouldn't believe it possible."

Clearly one of the soldiers felt much the same way.

"It's a trick!" roared a big, bulky soldier. "A lousy, stinking trick!"

Dropping from his borrowed horse Dusty advanced fast and unnoticed as the soldiers showed signs of agreeing with their companion. The race came to an end as the Indian pony loped over a line drawn in the dirt, coming in a good six lengths ahead of the lathered roan and showing no signs of distress.

"Look like we win," one of the Comanche braves told the soldiers. "You pay-um bets off now?"

"I'll be damned if I'll pay you!" the burly soldier answered, moving forward and knocking open the flap of his holster.

"You make-um bet," growled the Comanche. "Now you pay up. White soldier horse beaten good and plenty."

Dusty knew he must act, and quickly, if he hoped to prevent an open explosion of trouble. Inveterate gamblers, the Comanche braves would never permit the soldiers to leave without paying and a fight, even if it ended without somebody getting killed, must inevitably lead to further incidents.

Experience as a lawman had taught Dusty that the best way to handle such a situation was in prompt, definite, and, if possible, spectacular fashion. He figured that, all things taken into consideration, he possessed the way to do just the right sort of handling.

Darting forward Dusty bounded into the air as Tommy Okasi taught him and delivered a *mae tobi geri* forward jump kick. Normally such an attack would be aimed to strike its recipient's head or upper torso. Dusty varied the theme a little in that his left foot struck the soldier's shoulder and his right caught the Comanche on the upper arm. Coming so unexpectedly added force to the power of impact and shot both men staggering to crash to the ground. Dusty landed back on his feet and swung to face the rest of the soldiers, leaving handling the Comanches to Long Walker.

"Back off!" the small Texan roared.

Such was Dusty's inborn power to command that he brought the soldiers to a halt. None of them could figure out just who Dusty might be, but they knew full well *what* he was. Being men with a few years of Army service behind them, all recognized the small Texan's tone; that of a tough officer backing the authority vested in him by the *Manual of Field Regulations* with a pair of hard fists. True, the intruder did not wear a uniform, but officers occasionally did walk out in civilian clothes and some even adopted the dress of a working cowhand; although few wore it in the manner born, as did the man before them.

A barked command from Long Walker drew the eyes of the braves his way. They belonged to the Pehnane band and knew their chief did not lightly take to having his orders ignored. Before any of the braves could decide what to do, something happened to draw them and the soldiers' thoughts away from hostilities against each other.

Letting out a snarl of rage the burly soldier rose and diverted his anger from the Comanche to Dusty. Apparently the soldier was so furious that he failed to see the danger, for he rushed at the small Texan in a bull-like charge. Dusty waited in a slightly crouched position the Kid knew all too well, but which the soldier failed to recognize. Out stabbed the small Texan's hands, catching the man's right wrist. Pivoting until his back halted the soldier's rush, Dusty used the *kata-seoi* one-side shoulder throw; a most impressive method in that it sent the one receiving it sailing over the giver's shoulder and deposited him flat on his back some distance from where he took off.

Just as angry at being attacked the Comanche bounced erect, jerked the knife from its sheath, and charged forward in the hope that the Texan found himself too busy handling the soldier to notice the fresh danger.

"Magic Hands!" yelled Long Walker, conscious that he could not arrive in time to help Dusty and surprised that his grandson refrained from taking a hand.

Turning, Dusty saw his danger and acted on it with commendable speed. Up swung the Comanche's knife and drove down again. Dusty lunged aside, avoiding the blow. Landing on his hands and left knee he drove the right leg in a roundhouse kick into the man's belly. Even as pain knifed into the Comanche and the breath gushed from his lips, Dusty placed the foot against his rump and shoved hard. Shooting forward, his knife having fallen when the boot landed, the Indian crashed to the ground and lay gasping in an attempt to regain his kick-ejected breath.

Without a glance at his two attackers Dusty bounded to his feet. He swung toward the remainder of the soldiers.

"What's all this about?" he barked.

Only with an obvious effort did the men manage to

tear their eyes from their still recumbent companion. Bully Taylor had quite a reputation as a fighting man and anybody who could flatten him with such ease deserved attention and respect.

"This here bunch of Injuns got talking about hoss racing to us—sir," the only noncom, a corporal, replied.

"How?" demanded Dusty before the corporal could go further.

"How?" repeated the noncom.

"The Indian camp and area is off limits to all soldiers," Dusty pointed out in a chilling tone.

Taking a legal stand in the matter seemed like the best way to follow up the advantage gained by showing his physical superiority. So it proved. Under Dusty's coldly accusing eyes none of the soldiers could start to think up a suitable explanation for their disobedience of a strict ruling laid down by their commanding officer. Glaring at the men in the manner of a martinet officer determined to maintain discipline, Dusty told the corporal to finish his excuse and make it good.

"We're on wood detail, sir," the noncom answered. "Met this bunch here and got to talking. Started joshing them about that ugly little hoss and when they told us it could run—Well, sir, just take a look at it—"

Despite the gravity of the situation Dusty could not help smiling inwardly at the corporal and soldiers' attitudes. Outwardly, however, he retained his grim, unsmiling attitude. Discipline in the U.S. Army tended to be enforced by painful methods, especially on a frontier post. So none of the soldiers wished to antagonize him, not knowing what rank he held or caring to chance asking about it.

"I'm still listening," Dusty said.

"We talked some more, sir, and the Indians wanted to bet that their hoss had the legs of anything we could show. Hell, sir, we couldn't miss a chance like that!"

"Only, you lost." Dusty reminded him.

"Yes, sir," admitted the corporal.

"And don't want to pay off. That's about what I'd expect of the Eighth Cavalry," sniffed Dusty, and swung toward where the Kid and Long Walker sat their horses in the background. "You, Scout, tell the chief that his men have cheated U.S.—"

"Asking the—your pardon, sir," the corporal put in.

"Wait until I've dealt with the chief, Corporal!" Dusty barked. "I'll order him to have the bets called off."

A low mutter of protest came from the listening soldiers; just as Dusty expected it would. While the soldiers might consider they were the victims of a trick, all knew it had come about through their own making. Dusty's comment about the Eighth Cavalry's lack of sporting qualities had been made deliberately. Knowing he had no authority to order the bets be paid—and realizing the consequences if the soldiers welshed on the wagers—Dusty used devious methods to achieve his ends. No soldier would want a man who apparently belonged to some rival outfit witness him perform an act of poor sportsmanship.

"We want to pay off the bets, sir," one man stated.

"Sure we do," agreed another and the remainder rumbled assent.

"What did you bet?" Dusty asked.

"Small things, sir. Watches, rings, bandanas," the corporal replied. "We'd not bet guns or anything like that."

"Did the Indians ask you to?"

"No, sir."

"You wanting me to tell the chief anything, Cap'n?" asked the Kid.

"Tell him that my men will pay their bets," Dusty answered. "And when you've done it, Corporal, I suggest that you get on with your detail. By the Great Horned Toad, if I had you in my outfit . . ."

Dusty allowed the threat to trail away, giving the impression that at any minute he might decide his duty was to report the affair.

While the soldiers paid off their wagers, including the man Dusty had made peace with, Long Walker growled Comanche advice to the braves. Although the buck who had tried to knife Dusty looked a mite sullen, he saw the wisdom of not trying further conclusions with Magic Hands of legendary fame. However, Dusty wanted to avoid giving the impression of siding with the Indians against his own kind.

"Does that chief speak English, Scout?" he barked.

"Just a mite, Cap'n," replied the Kid, catching on to the play and following Dusty's lead.

"Then tell him that I consider this whole fuss is the fault of his braves. I hold him responsible for the whole affair."

"I'll do just that, Cap'n," promised the Kid, and proceeded to spout his fluent Comanche in his grandfather's direction, sticking to what Dusty said in case any of the soldiers understood the language.

Give Long Walker full credit, thought Dusty, he acted just right. Looking reluctant to lay blame on his men, but unwilling to go against an influential member of the treaty council, the chief apologized through his "interpreter" and promised it would not happen again.

"See that it doesn't!" Dusty barked. "And take your men to their village."

Although that meant putting off the visit to the Waw'ai delegation, Dusty figured it must be done. He wanted to see the soldiers back into the fort and prevent the chance of further trouble. Acting as he had gave the men confidence in him, but he did not want to start them wondering why he did not demand the return of their property.

After Long Walker and his braves returned to the village, the corporal drew himself into a brace and saluted. Judging by the way that Indian-dark scout acted and addressed the small man, he held captain's rank. While one might occasionally play up a shavetail lieutenant, such a game did not pay when dealing with a full two-bar captain.

"About this, sir—" the noncom began, wondering what action the captain aimed to take against the private who had tried to attack him.

"I'd suggest that you forget it, Corporal, happen you want to keep those bars on your arm," Dusty answered. "The only reason I'm not taking action is that your colonel would court-martial you all for sure, and I'd hate to have it known that members of the U.S. Cavalry were hawg stupid enough to be suckered into a horse race."

"Reckon they'll do it, Dusty?" the Kid asked, watching the soldiers head back to the fort.

"I reckon they will," Dusty replied. "Anyways, I'll go back after them. Tell Long Walker I'll be along to talk with the chiefs tonight."

"It could have been bad," the Kid said soberly. "Happen the soldier started throwing lead, or that *tehnap* used the knife, both sides would have painted for war."

"That's for sure," Dusty drawled. "Thing being, Lon, was it just chance or did somebody set them soldiers up for it?"

CHAPTER EIGHT

THE PURPOSE OF THE LANCERS

Before Dusty or the Kid could form any conclusion on the averted trouble, a voice came to their ears.

"Hey, Dusty, Lon!"

Turning, they saw Mark Counter approaching and waited to learn what their amigo might be wanting.

"What's up, Mark?" Dusty asked.

"The stage's in, Temple's all right but the Waw'ai tried to jump him," Mark answered. "And General Handiman wants you pair back at the fort. He's got a few things to show you afore you go see the chiefs tonight."

"Who-all's come on the stage?" Dusty inquired as the three Texans started walking toward the fort.

"All of the committee except for Senator Rosenbalm. He missed the stage and won't be here for two days."

"Which means the council'll be delayed that much more," said the Kid.

Mark nodded to where the soldiers walked away and then to the departing Indians. "What's come off here?"

After explaining, Dusty went on, "I don't reckon anything to it."

"Or me," agreed Mark. "Those fellers who want to bust up the council couldn't've known the soldiers would meet a bunch of Indians who'd have the right sort of a hoss to fix that kind of race."

"Anybody who knows the Comanche'd know we like to gamble," the Kid pointed out.

"Sure, but they'd not lay plans on the chance of it coming off," replied Dusty. "And that soldier riding the Army horse wasn't trying to lose. Still, I reckon I'll ask the general to find out what he can about them. Anybody interesting on the stage, apart from Temple and the committee, Mark?"

"Senator Waterhouse brought his daughter along," Mark replied with a grin.

"Pretty gal?" inquired the Kid.

"Real pretty," admitted the blond giant. "Only, she don't like southerners in general and rich southerners least of all."

"Now, there's a gal with real good taste," drawled the Kid. "How's she on poor li'l quarter-Indian boys, you reckon?"

"Happen she's got the sense of a louse, which I doubt," Mark answered, "she'll run a country mile from them."

Passing through the fort area Dusty and his two companions approached General Handiman's temporary office. As they drew near the door, they heard the general making coarse comments on the subject of politicians. The comments chopped off as Dusty knocked and a gruff voice bawled for them to enter.

"Ah, Dusty," Handiman greeted, sitting at his desk with Lieutenant Manners standing at one side of it. "I want you, the Kid, and Mark to come with me. Somebody back East conceived the idea of sending a selection of our latest weapons out here to show the Comanche chiefs what they can do. Only, before I try it, I want to know which way the chiefs will be impressed."

"We'll take a look, then, General," Dusty answered.

"There's no rush. I'd like you to see them before you speak to the chiefs tonight, of course, but mainly I sent for you as an excuse to get away from those dog-blasted politicians. Do you know, Dusty, when I took this assignment I did it in the hope that I'd escape from politicians for a spell. Clean forgot that there'd be a bunch of them along—and that it's always the most pompous, overbearing kind who come on things like this."

"It looks like even generals have their troubles." Mark grinned.

"What rank did you hold in the war?" Handiman grunted.

"Lieutenant, Sheldon's Cavalry."

"Well, Mr. Counter," bristled Handiman, "you never saw the day as a shavetail lieutenant that you had a fiftieth of a general's worries. All you had to do was go out, get shot at, and likely get killed. Your general had the job of explaining why it happened to some—politician who was nowhere near when it happened and still knew more about it than the men on the spot did."

Having heard his uncle and other high-ranking staff officers of both sides on the subject of politicians, Dusty decided to head Handiman off before the general reached his full flow.

"About these fancy weapons, General," he prompted.

"Come along, I'll show them to you," Handiman replied.

Accompanied by Manners, who found himself assigned to act as the general's aide, Handiman led the Texans through the buildings to a locked, guarded stable-block on the edge of the parade square. After acknowledging the salute of the lancer who stood guard, Handiman took a key from his pocket, unlocked and opened the door, then allowed the Texans to enter. Dusty studied the line of weapons and decided that the U.S. government was going to considerable expense and trouble in order to impress the Comanche with the superiority of the white-eye brother's means of killing enemies.

"You know this one?" asked Handiman, approaching the nearest of the weapons.

"One of the new Gatlings, isn't it?" Dusty asked.

"An improved version," agreed Handiman. "Fifty caliber."

"A fair number of the chiefs saw that Ager during the war and it impressed them," Dusty said, looking at the five-barreled Gatling gun on its medium-artillery carriage and estimating its weight to be approaching half a ton taken with the ammunition caisson and actual weapon. "I reckon this might do it if you can show the chiefs how well it works."

"I reckon we might be able to do that," Handiman said. "We've brought in crack crews for all the weapons." He waved a hand to a small mortar mounted on a wooden bed, which had four carrying handles attached. "How about the Coehorn? Twenty-four pounder, twelve hundred yards range, light enough for four men to carry it into action."

"On hosses?" asked the Kid.

"How's that?" demanded Handiman.

"Can those four jaspers take it into a fight between 'em riding hosses?"

"It weighs two hundred and ninety-six pounds on the bed," Manners put in. "So they'd not be able to manage it from horseback."

"Then the Comanche won't be worried about it. They can haul down a village and start running faster than men on foot could move that thing up and use it."

"You wouldn't show it, then?" asked Handiman.

"How accurate is it?" Dusty put in.

"With a good team, which we have, very accurate."

"I'd show it then, General, only have it set up ready."

"You mean so that they don't see how slowly it takes to move it from place to place, Dusty?"

"That's it," grinned the small Texan.

"I saw some of these used one time," Mark put in, pointing to a metal box from which Manners lifted the next weapon. "It's a Hale rocket, isn't it?"

"A Hale spin-stabilized rocket with high-explosive head," corrected Manners, holding the projectile gingerly.

"And very dramatic too," Handiman went on.

Alongside the rocket box stood a metal tube five feet in length fitted with an adjustable rear sight and bipod legs. Dusty stepped forward and lifted the tube, recognizing it as a launcher for the rocket.

"More dramatic than effective, from what I heard," he said. "What do you reckon, Lon?"

"You could use a couple of rockets," the Kid replied. "The chiefs have seen cannon, but that'll be something new to them."

"So I thought," Handiman said. "What about the Whitworth rifle here?"

When Handiman used the term rifle, he meant the twelve-pounder breech-loading rifled cannon next to the rockets.

"It's field artillery," Manners went on, "and can keep up with the cavalry."

"Not fast enough to catch up to a bunch of Comanches when they decide not to fight," Dusty told him. "But you could show its range and accuracy, that ought to make an impression. The mountain howitzer there'll make a good showing too."

"Maybe even better than the Whitworth," Mark agreed.

On the face of it the comment might have seemed wrong. Stood alongside it the long-barreled Whitworth looked far more impressive than, and towered over, the thirty-three-inch tube, fifty-inch carriage, and thirty-eight-inch-diameter wheels of the mountain howitzer. However the little gun tossed a twelve-pounder shell and could be taken to pieces so as to be carried on a pack horse or mule—one animal carried the tube and shafts, another the carriage, wheels, and loading gear, while ammunition rode the packs of a third.

"The crew I've brought out for this gun can assemble it and get off an aimed shot in slightly under one minute," Handiman remarked.

While realizing the advantages of the mountain howitzer, the Kid said, "I've yet to see a pack hoss that could cover more than twenty miles a day toting that kind of load."

"So?" asked Handiman.

"An Injun village on the run'll cover thirty; bucks on their own—well, if they only go fifty miles they figure they've made poor time."

"It's still a mighty handy weapon," Dusty pointed out. "We don't have to tell the chiefs its limitations."

"You won't have to," replied the Kid.

For all that, he knew what impact the display of weapons would have upon the assembled Comanches. Shrewd warriors, with an inborn ability to judge the merits and capabilities of weapons, they would begin to realize the futility of fighting against such devices as the Whitworth rifled cannon that could hurl its charge accurately over distances well beyond any weapon the Indians possessed. Maybe those jaspers in Washington were smarter than he figured. They had certainly come up with a right convincing argument to present before his people for once.

"I'll tell the chiefs about the different weapons, General, but without letting them know we have them on hand," Dusty said. "Then you can arrange a display of them before the signing ceremony."

On leaving the stable Dusty's party found that the lancer guard was being relieved. A mounted lancer sergeant threw up a salute to the general, and his men stiffened to a brace.

"How about those lancers, General?" asked Mark. "Why're they here?"

"That's another part of the scheme to impress the Comanches," Handiman answered.

"Just how're they fixing to do that?" inquired the Kid.

"Somebody in Washington came up with the information that the Comanche treat a man who carries a lance as something special," explained Handiman. "So they sent Count Przewlocki's battalion out here to show the chiefs that we have lance carriers too. . . ."

"They're going to demonstrate their skill with the lance," Manners put in. "You should see them in action at tent pegging."

"What'd that be?" the Kid wanted to know.

"Sergeant!" Manners called, then looked at Handiman. "With the general's permission—?"

"Go ahead," Handiman assented.

"Have you a tent-pegging course laid out?" Manners asked when the sergeant rode up to him.

"Yes, sir."

"Then will you show these gentlemen how it is done?"

The sergeant, a slim man of Baltic extraction, barked an order to one of the sentries he had just relieved. Like all the men of his outfit he had served in a European lancer regiment and knew that most members of the U.S. cavalry had but small regard for the lance; which annoyed him. So he did not object to demonstrating a skill that lay beyond the capabilities of men not specially trained at the sport of tent pegging.

While the sergeant rode his horse along the edge of the parade ground, his sentry went to where a number of wooden pegs of the kind used for securing a tent's guy ropes lay. Taking a couple the soldier drove them into the ground some distance apart and before the spectators. After turning to face the pegs the sergeant set his horse moving at a slow gallop. His eyes studied the nearer peg and he measured his distance. Down lowered the lance, its tip spiking through the peg and withdrawing it from the ground. Swinging toward the general's party he raised the lance to show off the skewered peg; conscious that he had given a good demonstration.

"Well?" asked Manners, having tried tent pegging and learned that there was more to it than met the eye.

"Is that all?" the Kid countered.

"Could any of your Comanche lance carriers do it?"

While the Kid doubted if any Comanche worth his salt would use such a prized item as a war lance for that kind of display, he felt called on to uphold the honor of the Nemenuh. Turning, he looked to where his big white stallion stood before the general's office. As usual Shadow had not needed to be tied and so was free to answer its master's whistle. Running forward the Kid went up into the white's saddle in a single bound. From a fast trot, Shadow's pace increased to a racing gallop, and the Kid guided his mount toward the second of the pegs.

"What's he goi—" Manners began.

Drawing his bowie knife the Kid swung over and hung alongside his saddle. In passing he skewered up the peg with the same ease the sergeant showed; except that instead of a nine-foot-lance the Kid used the eleven-and-a-half-inch-long blade of the bowie knife, and his horse moved considerably faster than the soldier's mount. Not content with merely picking up the peg the Kid flicked it into the air and chopped it as it fell. So keen an edge did the great knife carry, that it sank into the end of the peg deep enough to hold the wood on the blade. Bringing the horse around in a rump-scraping turn, the Kid thundered down toward the watching men. He left the saddle while the stallion still ran at top speed, lighting down with cat-like agility before the open-mouthed, amazed-looking Manners.

"Didn't have a lance," the Kid drawled. "But I sure picked up that peg."

"But—" started Manners.

"Mister," interrupted the Kid. "Any Pehnane boy past ten summers could have done the same; only, without a saddle."

"You—you're joshing me," Manners said.

Once again the Kid whistled and his horse swung back toward him. Leaping into the saddle he gave a display of trick riding the like of which Manners had never seen equaled. The U.S. Cavalry had its share of trick riders, but

Manners grudgingly admitted that none of them could touch that Indian-dark Texan. After a few seconds Manners began to wonder if bringing the lancers West to overawe the Comanche had been such a good idea after all.

So apparently did General Handiman. While he realized that the Kid possessed greater equestrian skill than the average Comanche, the general guessed that many of the braves approached the dark-faced youngster in ability. Enough to make trying to impress them, using the lancers, uncertain and risky. Clearly the Kid did not regard the tent-pegging skill of the sergeant as anything special and most Comanches would feel much the same way.

"Where's Colonel Przewlocki, Sergeant?" Handiman asked.

Surprise flickered on the noncom's face for a moment. "He took the battalion, less the line guard under me, out as you ordered, sir."

"As I ordered?" Handiman barked.

"Yes, sir. The general ordered that the battalion go out to bring the Waw'ai here for the council."

No respecter of persons, apart from Ole Devil and Dusty, the Kid swung an angry face toward Handiman even as the general exchanged startled glances with Dusty and Manners.

"Why in hell did you do that?" demanded the Kid hotly. "Any Nemenuh who hasn't come in yet won't be coming. The only way you could make the Waw'ai come here'd be by force, and that means fighting with 'em."

"I know that," Handiman answered, so surprised by the news that he did not take offence at the Kid's words. "And I never gave such an order to Przewlocki."

"Then who—?" Dusty began.

"Now, there's a real good point," Mark went on.

"And one I aim to feel at," Handiman growled. "Who brought my orders, Sergeant?"

"I don't know, sir. The colonel came from his quarters with a sheet of paper in his hand and ordered the battalion to move out. I heard him telling Captain Azarin they were to follow Elk Creek toward Lovatt City and look for the Waw'ai village, then bring in the Indians."

"When did they leave?" asked Handiman.

"At half past seven, sir," Manners put in. "I saw them go and thought they merely rode out to drill."

"Why not let Lon and me ride after him, General?" Mark asked. "If you gave us a written order for his recall—"

"Not you, Mark," Dusty interrupted. "I reckon Colonel Przewlocki wouldn't recognize your writing, General?"

"There's no reason why he should," admitted Handiman.

"Then it'd be best if one of the fort's officers went with Lon."

"Or I could send Mr. Manners here with one of the fort's scouts," Handiman suggested. "There is the council tonight."

"I'd thought about that," Dusty told him. "It'd best be Lon, unless you're real sure about the scout you send. Happen you send the wrong man, he'll just lead Mr. Manners in circles and make sure they either don't find the lancers, or find them too late."

"I don't know the post staff," admitted Handiman. "Can you speak to the chiefs without the Kid being along, Dusty?"

"Sure. Lon's pappy made me his blood brother before we went to the Devil Gun council and I reckon it still holds good."

"It does," confirmed the Kid. "Once you're made a blood brother, only death can end it. I'll go see Grandpappy Long Walker and tell him what's happened. Want to borrow a good hoss from him too. See that you get something that can move, mister. We won't be letting grass grow under our feet."

"I'll see to it," promised Manners, a little haughtily.

"And don't go loading it down like you soldiers most times do when you put your noses outside the walls."

"We won't catch up to them today—," began Manners.

"That figures," said the Kid.

"Then how about food?"

"The only way we can catch up to them to do any good, mister," the Kid warned, "we won't have time to worry about it."

"Go make your arrangements, Mr. Manners," ordered Handiman. "And listen to the Kid. Take his advice in everything pertaining to finding Colonel Przewlocki *before* the lancers find the Waw'ai village."

CHAPTER NINE

MR. MANNERS SEES A CARACOLE

Four miles from the fort night came on so dark that the Kid could no longer read the sign of even so large a party as the Lancer detachment.

"Reckon we'd best night here," he said. "Could follow the stream until it joins the Elk Creek if you like."

They had been following the smaller stream that served the fort as water supply before joining Elk Creek and the Kid waited, showing remarkable tact, for Manners to make a reply. Sensing that the other displayed goodwill in even offering to share the decision, Manners shook his head.

"You're the one who's following the sign. The lancers might turn off and us not know until too late, though. I'd say bed down here."

On that note of friendly cooperation the Kid slid from the saddle of the big iron-gray horse borrowed from his grandfather. He had left his white stallion at the fort, knowing his two companions could care for Shadow's basic needs and that the horse needed a rest after the hard work done over the past weeks. Dismounting from the fine-looking bay charger, one of a pair presented to him by his family on his being sent West, Manners glanced at the Kid and then set to work attending to his horse's welfare.

Feeling almost naked without his bedroll, food supply, change of clothing, and all the other items the soldier—

or his horse—carried when on patrol, Manners wondered how the Kid expected them to exist until they caught up with the lancers. Fortunately they had both found time to eat a good meal before leaving the post, but that would hardly last for a day or more. From what Manners could see, the Kid did not appear to be worried by the lack of food. One thing the lieutenant noticed, the Kid clearly needed no supervision in matters of horse management.

"They'll do," the Kid drawled, when the horses had been cooled down, off-saddled, watered, and hobbled on good grazing.

Suddenly Manners realized that his companion regarded *him* as the one who might need supervising and the feeling irritated him. After all, he was a well-educated man, a product of the West Point Military Academy and a potential commander-in-chief of the U.S. Army. Yet that Indian-dark Texan who—

"How about lighting a fire?" Manners asked, fighting down his annoyance.

"I wouldn't," the Kid replied.

"But we're not in hostile territory," Manners objected.

"Anywhere's hostile to somebody," countered the Kid. "And a couple of good hosses'd make mighty fine pickings for some young buck, even happen he's headed for the peace council."

"How about cooking our food?" Manners said, suddenly conscious that he had failed to bring any supplies along.

"Grandma Maria gave me a couple of *awyaw:t* of pemmican," drawled the Kid. "It'll do us and don't need any cooking."

Like most soldiers on the frontier Manners was acquainted with pemmican. He knew many officers who regarded "Indian bread," as they called it, as a delicacy but had never grown to like it himself. However, he learned there was a vast difference between the hard, tasteless mass all too often traded by Indians to unsuspecting soldiers and the real pemmican put up by a Comanche squaw for home consumption. The Kid's grandmother, as became the *pairaivo*, could claim to be an artist in pemmican preparation, knowing how to mix the pounded, heat-softened meat, cherries, plums, pecans, pinons, walnuts, and chestnuts, merging the whole with tallow or marrow fat so that they blended and each added its own taste to a mouth-watering, delicious whole. Wrapped in the parfleche container known as an *awyaw:t*, the whole coated in melted tallow that hardened to form an airtight seal, the pemmican could be stored for almost indefinite periods.

"This is good," Manners praised, carrying a second slab after finishing the first.

"Grandma Maria knows how it's done," admitted the Kid. "Tastes better with honey smeared on, though. When we was up in the Cross Timbers country we'd find the bees' nests—don't ask me why, but there were more there than in any other area we knew—put the honey in skin bags and use it on the pemmican."

"It's good even—" began the young officer and stopped as the Kid made a silencing gesture.

For a few seconds the Kid sat, his head cocked slightly on one side, looking like a hound dog trying to locate some distant, half-heard sound. At last he looked at Manners and said, "Somebody's riding by down that ways."

"The lancers?"

"Nope. Half a dozen of 'em at most and going away from the fort."

"Who could that be?" Manners asked before he could stop himself.

"Not soldiers, that's for sure," drawled the Kid. "They're traveling too quiet and like they know where they're going."

Before Manners could make a reply to the comments on Army ability, the Kid stretched out on the ground and used his ears once more. The young officer kept perfectly still, knowing what his companion hoped to do. Although he strained his ears, Manners could not detect any sound other than the usual night noises. Lifting his head, the Kid looked at the officer.

"Like I said. Six of 'em, riding unshod hosses. Likely a bunch of bucks going back to the village. Not every *tehnap* came in, and the ones still out'll want to know what's going on."

"Is that all they'll be doing?"

"I don't reckon they'll be painted for war, or even raiding. There's no way we can find out anyways. Let's get some sleep, we've a hard day's riding ahead of us afore we catch up with the lancers."

Although Manners felt that he should be doing something about the departing Indians, he could not think what. So he settled down and tried to make himself as comfortable as possible with only a saddle for a pillow and two blankets to replace sheets and mattress as a bed. Much to his surprise he did fall asleep, and nothing woke him before dawn began to creep on the eastern skyline. It seemed to Manners that the Kid had also slept well and the young officer did not know that twice during the night his companion awoke to listen to small groups of riders passing in the same general direction taken by the first party.

After eating pemmican, washed down by stream water, the Kid and Manners rode on. Tracking proved to be no difficulty and at first the lancers followed Elk Creek's winding course. Manners noticed that the Kid seemed unusually silent and alert, but asked no questions. If it came to point, Manners found no time to ask. While he thought of himself as a skilled horseman, he rode with a master long used to extensive, fast travel and needed all his ability to keep up with the Kid.

Four hours of hard riding brought them to where the lancers had made camp for the night. Even without the

Kid's help Manners could see that the men they followed had left the creek on moving out at dawn. The lancers' tracks led off across the open range, but the Kid did not start along the new line straightaway. Leaving the horses to rest he circled the area on foot. When he rejoined the officer, he looked serious and disturbed.

"Feller met up with them just afore they made camp last night," he said. "He came up from the way they're going now."

"It could be their scout and he's found something," guessed Manners. "And if I'm right, we'd best catch up."

"And quick," agreed the Kid, walking to his horse. "They pulled out at about the same time as us. We're going to have to push these hosses, mister."

Once clear of the river they rode through rolling, open range dotted with clumps of bushes or trees and gashed by gullies, dried-up watercourses, and hollows. While not slowing the pace any, the Kid tried to follow a route that kept them out of plain sight as much as possible, and Manners found himself admiring the other's success in doing so. They saw no sign of the lancers, nor was the range's surface conducive to producing a dust cloud that might lead them to their goal. Underfoot the close-cropped buffalo grass held in firm soil that did not pulverize and churn into the air. It was ideal cattle country and offered a home for a type of animal found only on the plains of the United States.

Starting ahead in the hope of locating some sign of the lancers, Manners saw first one, then more flickers of white about three quarters of a mile ahead and far too scattered for them to be caused by the sun glinting on lance heads.

"Over this way!" snapped the Kid before Manners could ask a question, and led the way into a small draw with bushes along its rim.

Dropping from their saddles the two young men moved to the top of the draw and peered cautiously through the bushes. Manners held a pair of field glasses he brought along and glanced at the Kid before offering to use them. After studying the position of the sun, to make sure that its rays would not be reflected from the glasses' lens, the Kid nodded his agreement. Focusing his glasses Manners quickly found the cause of the flashing, although he had already guessed, correctly, at its source.

"Pronghorns flashing," he said casually, attaching no great importance to the discovery and wondering at why it caused such a reaction from the Kid.

"What's making 'em flash?"

"Huh?"

"They only do it when they're spooked by something and want to warn their pards of trouble coming."

Antilocapra americana, the pronghorn antelope, was in many ways a unique creature, which possessed a number of unusual traits. Not the least interesting was its habit of "flashing." Controlled by a pair of muscular disks the circular white patch of hair on its rump could be erected in an abrupt manner that caused the light to reflect in a heliographic manner. On spotting danger a pronghorn would erect its hair and flash a warning to be taken up and repeated by other members of its herd until all received the warning and the plains seemed to be dotted with the flickering spots of light.

However, as the Kid pointed out, the pronghorn only flashed in times of danger. There were a number of animals that the pronghorn might regard as dangerous; with man standing high on the list. With that thought in mind Manners lay concealed among the bitterbush and scanned the range around the pronghorn as they started to run toward his hiding place. Even without artificial aids to sight the Kid beat Manners to the discovery. He knew from the escape route taken that the pronghorn had not been flashing warning of his and Manners's presence and guessed at the right place to look.

"Over there," the Kid said. "Coming down that dry wash by those half-dozen scrub-oak trees."

Turning his glasses in the desired direction Manners gave a low gasp. Some dozen Indians rode in single file down the dry wash and wended their way across the plain.

"Are they Comanche?" he breathed, although at that distance there could be no need to whisper.

Taking the glasses the Kid gave a closer study to the Indians and shook his head. "Nope. Kiowa."

"On a war trail?"

"They're not painted for it, anyways. Best way to tell'd be look at their arrows, though."

"How's that? I've heard the scouts say an Indian used war arrows, but they never explained."

The Kid broke a twig from the bush at his side and used it to illustrate his point. "You know how the feathers are fixed. Well, a hunting arrow always has its head fitted so that it stands straight up when it's on the bow. A war arrow's head is always crossways."

"Why? To make it harder to remove?"

"Nope. Easier to go in. A hunting arrow's for use against deer, elk, buffalo, and they stand on four legs. Their ribs are most time straight up from the ground. A man stands on two legs, his ribs are level with it."

Once explained Manners saw the whole thing and felt surprised that the primitive Indians would know such a thing or be able to deduce the difference between the normal standing position of human and animal ribs.

"What do we do?" the officer asked.

"Keep moving. They're headed in the same direction that we are, so we'll have to ride careful."

By staying in cover the two young men managed to continue their journey and avoid being seen by the Indians. Although they could no longer stick to the lancers' tracks, the Kid found no difficulty at first in following the correct line. Indian-wise he watched everything and had seen other significant tracks all going in the same general direction. All too well he knew what the gathering of the small bands of Indians meant.

Unless the Kid sadly missed his guess, the lancers were riding into just about the worst kind of trouble—and with the most inadequate armament any U.S. Army outfit had carried since the days before the Colt Dragoon brought repeating firepower to their aid.

Following a circuitous route and moving faster than the Kiowa, the Kid and Manners drew ahead. Then they reached a dead end, or rather a sheer drop, which brought them to a halt. Spread before the two white men, with a hundred-foot cliff dropping down to it, lay Wide Valley. Sitting their horses among the rabbit-bush clumps that scattered along the cliff top, the Kid and Manners stared down with the sickening knowledge that they had failed in their mission. The valley spread wide and almost as level as a racetrack. Out in the center of the valley Przewlocki's lancers halted in ten lines of ten men, their officers before them, watching Billy Salmon ride toward the mass mounted Waw'ai bucks who faced them at a distance of just over a quarter of a mile. The lancers made a brave, inspiring sight as the sun glinted on their lance blades and the pennants fluttered in the breeze. Yet all they did to the Kid was fill him with a sense of foreboding. Even before either he or Manners could make a move, they saw themselves to be utterly and irrevocably too late.

Sick with anxiety Billy Salmon rode forward to deliver Przewlocki's ultimatum to Sidewinder. Although the scout tried to plead a lame horse, Przewlocki refused to be deprived of his services. Rather than ride double Salmon stuck to his own horse and took comfort in the knowledge that his usefulness to the Death Bringer should save him.

Even as Salmon began to deliver a warning and demand that the Waw'ai accompanied the lancers to Fort

Sorrel, he saw Sidewinder bring up the Winchester carbine that was the chief's favorite war weapon. Shock stabbed into the scout, to be driven into the background of importance as he felt the sickening impact of a bullet. It seemed that Sidewinder had decided to wait no longer before collecting the much-coveted Army Colt.

So suddenly and unexpectedly did Sidewinder move that Colonel Count Ivan Mikola Przewlocki just sat and stared. Then, as his scout's body tumbled to the ground, he gave the order to charge and, saber in hand—officers did not carry a lance—led his men to the waiting Waw'ai.

This was the moment for which Przewlocki had waited and trained his men, when they would prove themselves in action. All opposition to his plans would be swept aside when he brought in a beaten village of Comanches and he could raise his regiment at the government's expense. With the support of a full regiment he could roam the Great Plains and select a suitable piece of land on which to establish a ranch. The weight of public opinion would ensure that the hero of Indian campaigns received his just rewards, of that he felt sure. There would be other benefits; not the least of which were large numbers of Indian horses taken as loot from captured villages, to form the nucleus of his ranch's stock. However, first he must deal with the Waw'ai, least respected fighters of the Comanche Nation.

Holding his men in the same tight formation so as to present a solid block of lances rather than a single line, Przewlocki saw the Waw'ai coming to meet him. The sight did not worry him, for his men rode big horses and could smash through their opposition by sheer weight.

Up on the rim top Manners stared in fascination and kept silent. At his side the Kid swung up the Winchester rifle. Although he could not recognize his childhood enemy, the Kid knew that war bonnet chief leading the Waw'ai must be Sidewinder. Yet the dark young Texan did not shoot. Despite its manufacturer's advertising claims, the Winchester Model 1866 lacked accuracy at any but short range. Over half a mile separated the Kid from Sidewinder, and at that distance only pure luck would bring a hit, especially when shooting downward and against a tricky crosswind. Maybe the Kid would have taken his chance and hoped that Ka-Dih looked on with favor, but a movement caught the corner of his eye. Once he located the cause of the movement, he knew he must not fire if he hoped to take news of Przewlocki's fate back to Fort Sorrel.

The drumming thunder of hooves filled the air, mingled with the war whoops of the Waw'ai and echoing back from the walls of the cliff. Closer came the two parties on what looked like a collision course. Down swung the lances into line, the eleven-inch-long, triple-edged blades designed to pass through a tent peg, or human flesh, with the least resistance. Soon, or so it seemed, the lances would be feeling Comanche blood.

Then, at the last moment, the solid wall of Waw'ai split, horses whirling and carrying their riders to safety. Separating into two groups the Waw'ai shot off to the flanks of the lancers and cut loose with a hail of bullets or arrows. Down went lancers and their mounts under the remorseless storm of death-bringing missiles. The white men backing Fire Dancer had been lavish in presents of repeating rifles, ammunition, and arrows, which, although manufactured by machinery back East, carried steel heads as lethal as any that came from the hands of the most experienced Comanche *tsukup*.

Przewlocki found himself faced with a serious problem. If he tried to halt the charging horses, he would throw his command into utter confusion. So he took the only way out in trying to continue through the two groups of enemy: reform and meet them on the other side. A savage face, hideously barred in scarlet paint, flickered momentarily before Przewlocki and flame tore from a rifle barrel. Searing pain ripped into the colonel and he slid slowly out of his saddle. A moment later the hooves of his men's horses churned over him, but he did not feel them.

Two minutes after the charge should have made its contact, Przewlocki's lancers ceased to exist as an organized fighting body. The valley bottom became dotted with still blue-clad shapes, while fleeing soldiers discarded their lances so as to be the better able to escape.

"Did you see that?" gasped Manners, his sole attention focused on the valley bottom and his heart filled with sick anxiety. "Those Indians performed a perfect caracole."

"A what?" asked the Kid, darting glances all around him.

"A caracole. It's the oldest known cavalry maneuver."

"Is it?" drawled the Kid. "We've been using it for years."

"Let's get down there and help!" Manners suggested as Przewlocki was shot.

"How?" demanded the Kid. "We're not the only ones watching. Look along the rim a piece."

Following the direction of the Kid's gaze Manners felt as if a cold hand had touched the base of his spine. Not half a mile away the group of Kiowa braves seen earlier that day sat their horses and watched the fight.

"How long have they been there?" gasped the lieutenant, forgetting his surprise at having seen a band of savages perform a classic cavalry tactic.

"Near on as long as we have," the Kid replied. "And now we've got to get the hell out of here."

"How about the lancers?"

"There's nothing we can do for them now. They'll have to take their chances the same as we will. Mister, that fight down there could blow up the whole damned peace council. We've got to head back to Sorrel, grab us some help, then come and whip the hell out of those Waw'ai. And we've got to do it now, afore them Kiowa stop us."

"They haven't interfered with us yet," objected Manners.

"Nope," agreed the Kid. "They've been waiting to see which way the fight down there went. Well, now they've seen, and we'd best go."

Although Manners knew the Kid spoke the truth, it went against the grain to desert men at such a time. Yet there did not appear to be a thing two men might accomplish against the Waw'ai, especially from the top of a sheer cliff and while faced with the opposition of a large bunch of armed Kiowa.

"But—" Manners began.

"You can come or stay," warned the Kid. "I know what I *have* to do, and I'm going to do it."

With that the Kid turned his horse and started it moving. Much as he hated to pull out, he knew it to be the only way. So did Manners. Swinging his mount the lieutenant urged it after the Kid and the two of them set off across the range at a slow gallop. Manners rode with the sick sensation of failure on him, for he had failed to reach the lancers in time and the outcome of the peace council hung precariously in the balance.

CHAPTER TEN

NO TIME FOR GENTLE METHODS

Miss Cornelia Waterhouse was a serious-minded young lady who had the misfortune to be very pretty, very shapely, and very attractive to members of the opposite sex. So much so that she often found difficulty in persuading young men of her true nature. Certainly the young officers at Fort Sorrel failed to appreciate her and showed little desire to join in sober discussions as to the countrywide implications of the treaty council.

Being serious minded, Cornelia felt compassion for the mass of humanity less fortunate than herself in the matter of worldly goods and social position. Her heart went out to the poorer classes and she wanted to help them achieve better conditions in life.

At times, it must be admitted, she wondered if perhaps her efforts fell on barren ground. Attending a social function organized by a friend's father for his workers, she overheard a number of comments on her motives for being present, few of which were complimentary. However, her select group of intensely intellectual friends explained that such often happened and laid the blame on bosses' spies making trouble and preventing the other workers from seeing the light. Which hardly made up for her having heard at least three different members of the crowd asking, "Why the hell doesn't she go back to her own kind and let us have our fun?"

Nor had her efforts to integrate the white and colored

workers met with any better success. In fact one white worker had the audacity to remark that she might advocate allowing an unlimited number of negroes to come North in search of employment as their presence could not affect her in any way. Fortunately such bigots were few and far between, for Cornelia, like most intellectual do-gooders, hated to have to face the truth.

All in all she felt grateful when her father brought her along with him to the treaty council. He held his seat in Congress on the strength of the workers' votes, and her views on a number of matters proved embarrassing; which may have accounted for his offer.

To Cornelia the trip offered an opportunity to study conditions in Texas and make the acquaintance of the downtrodden Indians. After the first night at the fort she found herself at a loose end. Her father was already involved in the first of the party policy rows that would plague the council. Having heard enough the previous night to warn them off, even such young officers who had no specific duty that morning avoided the girl and she did not trust Texas-born, southern-raised Dusty Fog, Mark Counter, or Temple Houston. So she walked alone from the fort toward the Comanche camps.

During dinner in the officers' mess the previous evening, before he went out to deliver a stirring address to the assembled chiefs, Dusty Fog had mentioned that any member of the party who wished to visit the Comanche would receive courtesy and be safe among the Pehnane. Suspecting that Dusty must have an ulterior motive for his suggestion, the girl ignored perfectly sound advice and directed her footsteps toward the tepees of the Kweharehnuh. Miffles, her poodle, bounded along before her, for she had not felt it safe to leave the little dog in a position where that brutal Temple Houston could allow his savage hound to attack it.

To reach the Kweharehnuh camp Cornelia had to pass through a large patch of wooded country, but found a fairly wide track and followed it. Going ahead of its mistress the poodle caught a scent of interest and went to investigate it. Cornelia let out a cluck of annoyance and followed her dog, calling to it. Passing through a clump of bushes she came face to face with two white men. A western-raised girl, or even one born in less favorable circumstances back East, would have taken one glance at the men, noted their menacing attitudes, and got the hell out of it. Cornelia saw only a tall, unshaven man in range clothes and one of medium height who wore a town suit of sober hue.

"Hello," she said brightly, but felt a little disconcerted by the way the taller man scowled at her. "My dog came—"

"How long have you been around here?" the bigger man growled.

"You have to excuse Mr. Higgins, my dear young lady," his companion said in a much milder tone. "Your appearance startled us."

"I'm sorry," Cornelia apologized. "But my little dog— Miffles. Come here!"

The latter command rapped out as Miffles darted between the two men and around the trunk of the flowering dogwood tree under which they stood. Knowing that obedience was not the poodle's greatest virtue, Cornelia swooped after it around the trunk and found the dog standing hopefully licking the top of one of several stone jugs that had so far been hidden from her view. Some instinct caused the girl to turn around and she found the men approaching her. A feeling of near panic bit into Cornelia at the raw fury on the big man's face. Yet Higgins's companion filled her with a greater horror as he spoke. While his voice remained the same, it held undertones of menace.

"You shouldn't have seen those, young lady," he told her mildly.

"We can't let her go, Bristow!" Higgins pointed out.

"I—I don't understand!" gasped the girl.

"I do."

Never had Cornelia expected to feel pleasure at hearing the voice of a rich southerner, or to experience delight at seeing one of the Confederate war heroes. Yet those two words and the sight of Dusty Fog and Mark Counter standing in the background gave her the most pleasant experience of her life.

On returning from tending to their horses Dusty and Mark had seen the girl leaving the fort. From the direction she took, and remembering certain remarks she had made the previous evening, the Texans guessed at her destination. While she would be safe under Long Walker's care, the girl had to reach the chief first, and Dusty recalled his experience at the hands of the *tuivitsi*. Should anything untoward occur to the girl in the Pehnane village it could cause repercussions that might affect the whole council. So the Texans followed Cornelia at a discreet distance and knew they had done the right thing when she headed not to the comparative safety of the Pehnane but toward the tepees of the Kweharehnuh, the least friendly band present.

Before the Texans could catch up with her and suggest that she go to the Pehnane village, Cornelia disappeared among the bushes. On following her Dusty and Mark needed only one glance at the stone jugs to know what Bristow's words meant.

At the sound of Dusty's voice the two men with Cornelia swung around. While Higgins's right hand went toward the gun holstered at his side, his left closed on the girl's arm and started to draw her toward him. Through horrified eyes Cornelia saw Dusty's left hand begin to move. Somehow, she could not guess how, the small Texan held a Colt, its barrel lined toward her, and flame tore from its barrel.

Seeing Higgins's move, Dusty did not dare hesitate. If the man once pulled the girl before him, he could use her as a shield or hostage. So Dusty drew and fired in the only way he could, for an instant kill. Lead ripped into Higgins's head and slammed him backward; his gun half drawn and left hand jerking away from the girl's arm.

Thinking that both the Texans might be concentrating on Higgins, Bristow made a move in the direction of his gun. He froze as he found out his mistake and saw the right-side Colt scooped from Mark's holster in a move almost as fast as the one with which Dusty had ended Higgins's life. While he faced a hanging charge for his action, previous to the arrival of the girl, Bristow lived by the old saying that while there was life there was also hope. Should he try to complete his draw in the face of the blond giant's obvious mastery of the gun, he would have neither hope nor life for long.

"Throw it away!" Mark ordered, and Bristow obeyed, tossing his gun aside in a careful manner that gave no offence to the watching Texan.

Cornelia stared first at Dusty, eyes on the Colt, which dribbled smoke in his right hand. Then she looked down at Higgins, seeing the blood that trickled from the hole in his forehead.

"You—you killed him!" she gasped.

"Yes, ma'am," agreed Dusty flatly.

"You killed him!" repeated the girl, her voice rising a couple of notes.

This time Dusty ignored her, his eyes on Bristow as he and Mark drew closer to the man. "All right!" Dusty growled. "How much of it have you sold?"

"What's that supp—" Bristow began.

Dusty knew a number of legal ways of interrogating a suspect but time did not permit him to use them. Around lashed his free hand in a slap that caught the man's face and spun him around to crash into the tree trunk. Bristow could not hold back a croak of pain as Dusty's knuckles caught him, and he knew that his troubles had only just begun.

Having served as Dusty's first deputy Mark knew that the small Texan did not normally employ such tactics to gain information. He also knew why Dusty acted in such a manner and heartily approved of it under the circumstances. Those stone jugs contained enough concentrated trouble to blow the whole peace council into the air and stir up a good-sized Indian war. With that in mind Mark holstered his Colt and stepped forward. He caught Bristow's right wrist in his big right hand, forcing the arm up behind the man's back in an agonizing manner. Nor did Mark content himself just with that. Steel-hard fingers clamped hold of the back of Bristow's head and forced his features savagely against the hard bark of the tree.

"Where's the rest of your booze?" the blond giant demanded.

Horror twisted Cornelia's face as she watched the agony contort Bristow's struggling body. With her head full of hatred for southerners and ideas about the sanctity of human life, she ignored the fact that Dusty had saved her life. Probably she did not know just how grave her danger had been when the Texans put in their appearance. All she knew was that Dusty had killed one man and now seemed set to torture another.

"Stop!" she screamed. "Release him or I'll have you arrested."

Like most of her kind she professed the gravest distrust of peace officers yet did not fail to invoke the law's protection when needing it. However, her words might never have been said for all the notice the Texans took. Mark relaxed his hold of Bristow's head long enough to repeat the question and, on receiving no answer, once more forced the crushed, damaged features against the trunk.

Cornelia let out a gasp, turned, and stumbled blindly back toward the path with her poodle following her. In her distraught frame of mind she did not notice that she ran away from the fort instead of toward it. Rounding a corner she found herself faced by a trio of armed Comanche *tehnap*.

Once again Cornelia's inexperience showed. Any girl raised in the Texas range country would have known from the antelope hide clothing, as opposed to the more usual buckskins, that she faced Kweharehnuh Comanches. Not that a western girl would have wasted time worrying about which band the men belonged to on noting their general attitude and the thing one of the bucks held in his hand. Lacking a basic knowledge of such important facts Cornelia did not see her danger until too late.

Letting fall the stone jug he held, the center buck of the party sprang at the girl. As he caught her and began to drag the coat from her shoulders, Cornelia received a faceful of his breath. It almost made her gag, and she breathed in the fumes of a raw whiskey the like of which she had only smelled once before; when she and her friends went to picket a detachment of police who destroyed a cache of illegally brewed "red biddy" back East. Terror filled her and she began to scream.

Bow on its topknot or not, the little poodle gave a growl and sprang to its mistress's aid and sank sharp teeth into the Indian's ankle. With a bellow of rage the *tehnap* jerked his leg and sent the dog flying. One of his companions held a bow and, even though drunk, notched an arrow to the string in fast time. Even as he started to aim at the dog, the bowman heard the sound of approaching feet and swung to face the fresh menace. At his side the third Comanche brought up his Winchester carbine ready for use.

On hearing the girl's scream Dusty and Mark realized that she had left them and guessed what she had run into. At the same moment Bristow gave a low moan and went limp in Mark's hands. Releasing his hold Mark turned and dashed after Dusty in the direction of the scream. As soon as they had gone, Bristow raised his bloody face from the ground. Groaning a little he rose and darted into the bushes.

Bursting into sight of Cornelia and the Indians, Dusty and Mark missed death by inches. A bullet fanned by the small Texan's cheek, so close that its eerie *splat!* sound almost deafened him; but did not put him off his aim. Firing on the run Dusty shot the bowman an instant after an arrow winged its deadly way through the air. Mark felt the arrow brush his trousers as it passed between his legs just below the crotch. In echo to Dusty's shot he cut down on the third Comanche and his bullet drove home just as the brave worked the Winchester's lever, spinning him around then tumbling him to the ground.

Thrusting the girl aside the last buck snatched out his war weapon, a Dragoon Colt taken from a dead soldier's body after a long-forgotten brush with the cavalry. He looked as mean as a winter-starved grizzly bear and dangerous as a pitful of stirred-up rattlesnakes as he lunged forward. Dusty and Mark knew that a drunken Indian could not be reasoned with. So they did not try. Two Army Colts roared at the same instant, their bullets converging on the Indian, slamming into him and throwing him back to his heels. Even then he still retained his grip on the Dragoon and tried to use it. Without a single hesitation, acting in the manner of a trained lawman faced with the same situation, Dusty shot again and a third time. It took both bullets to finish the Kweharehnuh. The Dragoon clattered from a lifeless hand as the Indian crumpled and fell to the ground.

At the same moment Cornelia let out a gasp and slid down in a faint. For the first time since their arrival Dusty and Mark gave the girl attention. Not much, though, for they realized the seriousness of their position. As usual Dusty thought fast and rattled out his summing up of the situation.

"The bucks from the Kweharehnuh village'll be coming soon, Mark," he said. "You'd best take the gal back to the fort fast and warn the general to be ready for trouble. I'll collect that damned whiskey-peddler."

"Go to it," Mark replied.

Even as the blond giant scooped the girl up from the ground, showing no more strain than if she were as light as a newly born baby, he heard shouts in the direction of the Kweharehnuh village. Without wasting more time he started to stride out in the direction of the fort.

Once more Dusty plunged through the bushes, changing guns on the way. Although he found the clearing, there was no sign of Bristow.

"Damn it to hell!" Gusty growled. "He must've been playing possum."

Quickly Dusty studied the surrounding area. He could not claim to possess the Kid's skill at reading sign, but knew enough to see where Bristow had taken a hurried departure. Before Dusty started in pursuit, he took time to wrench the stopper from each bottle and upend the contents on to the ground. Leaving full containers of whiskey where the Indians might find them would have been as dangerous as laying down a fully loaded, cocked revolver in the presence of mischievous children. With that elementary precaution taken Dusty headed for the bushes in the direction taken by the fleeing Bristow.

Before the small Texan had gone many yards, he heard the drumming of hooves and rattle of rapidly turning wheels. Realizing the futility of pursuit on foot Dusty did not even try. Instead he ran through the bushes and trees toward the fort. A cowhand's boots had never been designed for work on foot, but Dusty made good time in his for all that.

As Dusty left the woods and came into sight of the fort, he saw Mark emerge still carrying the girl. However, Dusty did not give his friend a second glance, being far more interested in the procession that was filing out of the main gates. The events of the past few minutes had chased all thoughts of the proposed display of weapons from Dusty's mind. Seeing the various dignitaries approaching followed by first the Whitworth rifle then the other special weapons brought remembrance back to the small Texan. It also offered him a way to stop the departing wagon.

Unfortunately none of the approaching party rode a horse, a fact Dusty noticed with a low curse at his lousy luck. Normally the sergeant in command of the Whitworth rifle would have been mounted on a horse instead of walking alongside the limber; and on occasion the crew of the mountain howitzer rode into action. Wishing to avoid emphasizing the lack of mobility of the weapons, Handiman ruled that each gun would be in position ready to be shown and so avoid undue movement. Even the lancers, who could only ride into action, did not offer any solution, their part in the display having been canceled.

"That's my daughter!" Senator Waterhouse bawled, looking more than usual like a well-dressed and -fed sheep, staring toward Mark. "What's happened to her?"

"What the hell's going on, Dusty?" Handiman barked.

"There's been a whiskey peddler at work, General," Dusty said, "and he's escaping."

Handiman might be lacking in knowledge of Indians, but he could claim full awareness of how the red brother reacted when under the influence of paleface firewater. So, too, could all the soldiers involved in the display, if their expressions were anything to go on as they looked at Handiman and awaited his orders.

"Up there, General!" snapped the colonel commanding the fort, pointing to where a light wagon pulled by four horses came into sight and spun off along the trail in the opposite direction to the party. "I'll send a—"

"Stop that wagon Sergeant Pratt!" shouted Handiman, addressing the noncom in charge of the Whitworth.

Quickly the sergeant studied the situation, knowing his professional reputation depended on his handling of the assignment. Accurate the Whitworth might be, but it could not be traversed at speed; which made firing at a moving target crossing its front extremely difficult.

"I'll have to pick a better place, General, sir," he pronounced.

"Then do it!" Handiman ordered.

"Can I go along?" asked Dusty.

"Take Captain Fog with you, Sergeant," confirmed the general.

"You'll have to ride the off swing hoss, Cap'n," Pratt said.

Without the caisson following to carry the remainder of the crew, Pratt operated using only the drivers and three men who rode the limber. However his men did not need their personal belongings and so the valise-saddles of the offside horses carried no loads. Although far from comfortable the valise saddles offered a means of transport and Dusty swung afork the center horse on the right side. Taking his place on the off lead horse, Pratt gave the order to roll.

"What's happening, Mark?" asked Handiman as the Whitworth moved off.

"Miss Waterhouse run into a whiskey peddler in that bosque," Mark explained, setting the girl on her feet and allowing her to stagger into her father's arms. "We've got trouble, General; and, was I you, I'd get the Gatling set up ready and the civilians back inside the fort."

"Do it!" ordered Handiman, and looked once more at Mark.

"General!" Waterhouse put in before Handiman could speak. "My daughter—."

"You'd best get her into the fort, Senator," Mark interrupted. "Happen you don't want for her hair and yours to decorate some Kweharehnuh's scalp pole."

Working fast the Gatling gun crew swung their weapon so its barrels pointed toward the woods. Before the gun had been freed from its limber, the gunner stood at the firing handle and his number two brought a loaded magazine from the ammunition chest.

Give him credit, Waterhouse might be arrogant and pompous, but he possessed discretion. Seeing the martial preparations and realizing how exposed he would be in the event of hostilities, he took his daughter in his arms and headed toward the fort. Showing an equal grasp of the situation the rest of the congressional committee followed without waste of time.

"That's the first time I didn't have a politician ask questions," said the colonel dryly. "Shall I turn out the guard, General?"

"What's happened, Mark?" demanded Handiman, shelving the question until he knew more of the situation.

"Like I said," Mark answered, watching the woods. "The gal came across those whiskey peddlers and didn't like the way Dusty and me started asking questions. So she started for the fort, aiming to have us arrested, I'd say. Only she took the wrong turn and walked right into three Kweharehnuh bucks who'd beat us to the peddler."

"They didn't hurt her?" growled the colonel.

"She's scared, no more," Mark replied. "Dusty and me got there just in time. Only, you-all know what Indians are when they're carrying a gutful of Old Stump Blaster. When they're that way, you have to dissuade them fast and permanent."

"That's what the shooting was about," Handiman said bitterly.

"It was them, or us and the girl," Mark told him. "Which same if she'd been raped and killed you'd've had a war on your hands for sure."

"And we don't have one now?" asked Handiman, nodding to where a group of Kweharehnuh braves came from among the trees.

CHAPTER ELEVEN

A WORSENING SITUATION

Despite his considerable Civil War experience Dusty had never ridden into action on a field artillery vehicle and might have found the situation exhilarating under less trying conditions. Urged on by their drivers the six-horse team built up speed and Dusty found himself forced to concentrate on retaining his seat without the aid of stirrups while also avoiding attempting to steer the horse he sat. Going at a speed that almost equaled that of a ridden horse, the Whitworth's team tore along in the wake of the speeding wagon.

Scanning the winding trail ahead Pratt barked an order and the lead driver began to swing his horses in a turn. Smoothly and efficiently the swing and wheel pair followed and the pace slowered until the team came to a halt with the barrel of the Whitworth pointed toward the departing wagon. Even before the horses halted, the men on the limber deserted their seats. Swiftly two of the crew raised the gun's lunette from its retaining pin on the limber and by the time the limber moved the prescribed six yards away had slid a handspike into the pointing rings at the base of the stock.

After swinging down from his uncomfortable perch Dusty moved well clear so as to avoid impeding the work of what he could see to be a highly skilled team. There had never been a time in the war when the Confederates held ascendancy over the Federal artillery, and watching Pratt's gun crew, Dusty could see why.

In a remarkably short time the team had set the gun into line, fed one of the strange-looking hexagonal shaped shells, known as "bolts" and designed to ensure a gastight seal as well as engage in the rifling of the bore, and a one-and-three-quarter-pound firing charge into the breech. With a clang the breech block swung into position and the number-two man twirled the hinged screw-cap to lock it home.

Behind the gun Pratt aligned his sights. Not at the wagon, but on a corner around which it must turn if Bristow aimed to stick to the trail. Years of experience went into the move and the sergeant's mind clicked through a number of considerations. Calculating the wagon's speed, estimating the distance that the bolt must travel, time of ignition, wind velocity, and other items that affected the correct arrival of the shot, he manipulated the elevation screw and sighted the piece. Inside the breech reposed a percussion-ignited shell ready to explode on contact. All now depended on his ability to place the bolt in the right spot.

Satisfied that he could do no more, Pratt stepped clear and studied the wagon as it started to make the turn.

"Fire!" he ordered, waiting to observe the fall of the shot.

The number-four man tugged at the firing lanyard and the Whitworth roared, leaping backward under the force of the recoil. Springing from the positions they had adopted to avoid the gun's backlash, the crew prepared to return their piece to a firing line without waiting to see the result of the shot.

Unaware of his danger, but sure that pursuit of some kind would come, Bristow urged his wagon along at a full gallop. If he could reach Elk Creek before being overtaken, he hoped to pour all his whiskey into the water and destroy the evidence against him. With eastern politicians at the fort, summary justice would be less likely to be administered; even for the heinous crime of whiskey peddling. Given a chance at a trial he might even escape due to lack of evidence. Certain influential people would not want their part in his affairs brought to light and could be relied upon to do everything possible on his behalf.

Something hissed through the air, then Bristow heard the crack of an explosion behind him, accompanied by a lurch, and the rear of the wagon collapsed. His team swerved violently; glass and stone jugs shattered and the fumes of raw whiskey gushed into the air. In the distance Bristow heard the crack of a rifled cannon.

"That was some shooting, Sergeant!" Dusty enthused.

"It was lucky shooting," Pratt corrected with a grin; but he felt a touch of pleasure at receiving praise from a man of Dusty's caliber.

"Can I take a horse and get over there?" the small Texan went on. "I want that damned peddler."

"Use the near leader."

"If that feller up there shows fight from cover—"

"I'll give him another present," promised Pratt. "Bring up a solid shot."

Wishing to show the Whitworth's versatility Pratt carried solid ball, explosive, and canister loads in the limber's chest. Exchanging the explosive load for one of solid construction the number-five man delivered it to the gun. While that took place, Dusty went to collect his mount.

Artillery harness was designed to allow quick removal and replacement of dead or injured horses. Swiftly Dusty and the horse holder slid free the toggle fastenings from their links and released the left-side front animal. Then Dusty went into the saddle, scooped up the reins, and started his borrowed mount moving.

Dazed by suddenly finding himself under assault by a cannon, Bristow sprang down and glared wildly around.

One glance told him that he would be going no farther in the wagon. No cavalry accompanied the cannon, that he could see, so he might still make good his escape using one of the team horses. With that thought in mind, fear of the consequences lending speed to his limbs, he sprang toward the horses. While working he heard the drumming of approaching hooves and looked around to see Dusty charging across the range toward him. A snarl of rage broke from Bristow's lips. Long before he could unhitch a horse, that damned Texan would be on him. The butt of a Winchester rifle showed over the wagon's box, an ideal weapon when matched against a man armed only with revolvers.

Even as Bristow sprang to the wagon and grabbed the rifle, Dusty saw the danger and acted on it. The small Texan rode a route that kept him out of the Whitworth's line of fire and he did not hesitate in removing his Stetson and waving it over his head. Once more the cannon banged and a second bolt hurled at the wagon. It struck with savage force and, although it did not explode, produced a mighty effective result. Caught in the spray of wooden splinters hurled up by the impact, Bristow reeled away from the wagon. Tears filled his eyes and by the time he managed to clear them, Bristow saw Dusty thundering up. Colt in hand the small Texan brought the horse to a halt.

"Get flat on the ground!" Dusty ordered. "Keep your hands in plain sight. I'd as soon take you in dead as living, so it's your choice."

Having been in and around western towns most of his life, Bristow could tell a top-quality hand with a gun when he saw one. So he obeyed Dusty's orders without a single argument. While he doubted if the Texan aimed to shoot him on the slightest provocation, he felt disinclined to take the chance. One thing he did know, a man so fast and deadly accurate as Dusty had proved to be was not the kind to take chances with. So he lay face down and with arms spread out in plain view while the other disarmed him.

"Now get up!" Dusty commanded. "We're going back to the fort."

"I've got money in my wallet," hinted Bristow.

"You'll need it to hire a lawyer," Dusty answered, killing the hope. "Not that any kind of lawyer'll save your neck, hombre."

Mark Counter did not scare easily and had proved his courage a number of exacting ways. Yet in later years he would look back on the few minutes following Dusty's departure after Bristow as among the worst in his life. Standing watching the sullen-faced Kweharehnuh braves make their appearance at the edge of the trees, he felt like a man sitting in a room filled with open kegs of gunpowder while somebody tossed lit matches at them. At any moment the whole situation could blow up, and if it once did there would be no halting a full-scale battle.

It seemed that Handiman also read the signs correctly, for he barked, "Nobody draw a weapon. Gunner, you open fire only at my order!"

Already hands stole to holster flaps and the Gatling's gunner held the firing handle in a sweaty grip. If anything, the presence and apparent readiness of the Gatling held the Kweharehnuh in check. Constantly at war with the white man, their braves knew more than any other band about the weapons employed by the U.S. Army and a few of the older Model of 1862 Gatling guns had been used on Texas frontier posts. Seeing one of the deadly guns lined their way caused the braves to halt and hold conference. Yet Mark knew that one shot fired would start the assembled braves fighting back.

One of the braves turned and pointed to where a group of chiefs strode into sight. Instantly the remainder of the Kweharehnuh party relaxed and lowered their weapons.

"Long Walker!" Mark breathed. "Thank the Lord for that."

Taking in the scene Long Walker advanced. With so many old friends gathered about his fire and talking, the chief failed to hear the revolver shots and did not know there had been any trouble. One glance told him that something had gone wrong with the smooth running of the council and he moved forward. Leaving the rest of Long Walker's party the chiefs of the Kweharehnuh joined their braves.

"What is wrong, General?" asked Long Walker, giving for the first time a sign that he understood and spoke passable English.

"There's been bad trouble," Handiman replied. "Some of your—"

"Long Walker!" barked Dark Night, senior chief of the Kweharehnuh. "Three of our *tehnap* have been killed by the white men."

Exclamations rose from the other chiefs and they darted glances at the white men. Only Long Walker gave the impression of remaining impassive and he looked at Handiman.

"Is this true words, General?"

"Dusty and I killed them," Mark put in. "They were drunk and trying to harm the daughter of one of the white men from the East."

The first crack of the Whitworth sounded before anything more could be said and every eye swung in its direction. However, it and Bristow's wagon had passed out of sight over the horizon and so the white men could not tell whether the shot had been successful or not.

"Where did the *tehnap* get the firewater?" Long Walker asked, then repeated the words in Comanche for the benefit of the other chiefs.

"From a white man in the woods there," Mark explained. "We—!"

Again the Whitworth cracked and this time Handiman

knew he must tell the Indians why the cannon was being used.

"As soon as I heard, I sent a cannon to halt or destroy the whiskey peddler's wagon," he said. "Captain Fog went with the party."

"Then we must hope that Magic Hands has been successful," answered Long Walker. "This is bad, General."

"I know," Handiman replied.

One of the chiefs called to Long Walker and a conversation in Comanche began. While Mark did not speak the language, he guessed that views differed on the affair and wondered what Long Walker meant to do. At last the chiefs stopped talking, turned, and stalked away, with the exception of Long Walker. On joining their braves the Kweharehnuh chiefs spoke quietly and with some reluctance the braves turned to fade back among the bushes.

"The man who sold the whiskey will be punished, Long Walker," promised Handiman as the Pehnane leader walked toward him. "And the braves were in the wrong to attack the white woman. Will the chiefs come and see the weapon display?"

"Not today," Long Walker replied. "This trouble needs much talk, so we return to my tepee to make it. When we decide what to do, we will send word to you."

"But—!" Handiman began.

"He'll say no more, General," warned Mark as Long Walker swung around and followed the departing chiefs. "All we can do is wait and hope."

"If word of this gets out," the colonel remarked, "there's some who'll claim it's proof that the Comanche never really wanted peace."

"If they hadn't wanted it," Mark drawled, "they'd a mighty good excuse for painting for war."

"The colonel's with us in wanting peace, Mark," Handiman commented. "That's why we came here. Dismiss the weapon crews, Colonel, and make sure that nobody leaves the fort. One more incident will really fix us. I'm going back to my office. Are you coming, Mark?"

"I'll wait for Dusty and tell him what's come off," Mark replied, nodding to where the Whitworth's crew returned led by Dusty and a bound, dejected-looking prisoner. "Lordy lord, General, I'd've given anything for this not to have happened."

"So would I," Handiman agreed worriedly. "But it has and there's no going back on it."

On his return Dusty listened to the latest developments and said, "I'll go to the Pehnane village and see if they'll let me explain."

"You can try," Handiman replied. "They might be willing to listen to you. Is this him?"

"This's him," agreed Dusty, following the general's baleful gaze at Bristow. "What do you aim to do with him?"

"Sergeant of the guard!" barked Handiman. "Put the prisoner into solitary confinement and allow nobody to see him without *my* written authority."

Leaving the others Dusty walked in the direction of the Pehnane village. He saw the chiefs gathered before Long Walker's tepee and gained the impression that a heated discussion was taking place. However before Dusty could come anywhere near the circle of chiefs, he found his way blocked by a couple of Pehnane braves. Not *tuivitsi* in search of devilment, but mature *tehnap;* one, in fact, he recognized as War Club, the Kid's foster father. While neither man showed hostility, they appeared to be grimly determined to follow their orders.

"Turn back, Magic Hands," War Club ordered.

"I came to speak with Long Walker," Dusty answered.

"This is not the time."

Dusty knew that forcing a way by the two men would prove considerably harder than handling a group of hotheaded, unthinking young *tuivitsi;* even if doing so would be any answer to the problem. Accepting the Indian's statement Dusty gave up his intention of visiting Long Walker.

"Tell the chiefs that I have captured one of the men who sold the whiskey and killed his friend. The one I captured will be punished."

"That I will do," promised War Club.

Turning on his heel Dusty walked back to the fort. All too well he knew that the fate of the council—if not the peace between the white men and Comanche Nation —hung precariously in the balance. On reaching Handiman's office Dusty found a heated meeting in progress. Looking flushed and furious Waterhouse stalked up and down the office and his Republican companion stood glowering to where Handiman sat behind his desk. The two Democratic senators and Mark Counter were also present, although the blond giant stood apart from the politicians.

"What I want to know is why my daughter was allowed to go into danger!" Waterhouse was shouting as Dusty entered.

"Your daughter shouldn't have been out of the fort without an escort," Handiman replied. "Did she try to raise one?"

"I understood that all members of the senatorial committee could come and go as they pleased," Waterhouse snorted. "We were assured many times that there would be no danger."

"There wouldn't have been," Dusty put in, "if your daughter did as we suggested and confined her visits to the Pehnane."

"May I ask what your interest is in this affair, Captain Fog?" growled Waterhouse's companion, a die-hard Radical Republican who hated southerners on principle.

"The same as yours, I'd say," Dusty answered. "To make an acceptable peace with the Comanche."

"Why?"

"Because I've seen Indian wars and know what they

mean in suffering and human lives wasted. I'm not just doing it to score off on a political rival."

"Are you implying that I am?" bellowed the senator.

"Now, ease off, Senator," ordered Handiman. "Arguing among ourselves won't make matters any better. And I would point out that Miss Waterhouse owes her life to Captain Fog and Mr. Counter."

"I—I haven't thanked you gentlemen for saving Cornelia," Waterhouse put in, looking embarrassed. Yet, despite his political beliefs, he did feel extremely grateful to the two Texans for their part in saving his daughter. Cornelia had recovered enough to tell him what had happened and he knew that Dusty and Mark's intervention had saved her from a hideous fate.

"There's no call to thank us," Dusty drawled. "I'd've given anything to avoid the whole damned business, but it's too late for that now."

"It's lucky, in one way, that Miss Waterhouse went out there," Mark went on. "If she hadn't, the first sign we'd've had of those whiskey peddlers would've been when we got stirrup deep in drunken Indians."

That aspect of the affair had not struck Waterhouse and his anger at Cornelia being allowed into danger became tempered with the feeling that his daughter had taken a major part in preventing an even larger sale of liquor to the Comanche.

"There's some would say that the Comanche don't take this council seriously," Democratic Senator Houghton said. "Their braves get drunk—"

"Getting drunk's not confined to Indians, Senator," Dusty reminded him. "The one we want to blame is that jasper who brought the whiskey here."

"Did you see Long Walker, Dustine?" Handiman asked, hoping to divert the other men and prevent friction.

"No."

"So our friendly chief wouldn't see you," sniffed Houghton.

"He's talking with the other chiefs, Senator," Dusty replied. "When Long Walker's got something to tell us, he'll come and do it."

Not until shortly before sundown did Long Walker make an appearance. Dusty had seen and interviewed Bristow, using more formal methods than on the previous occasion. While sure that the man had been brought in as part of a plan to disrupt the council, Dusty could gain no proof. Clearly Bristow felt he had no great cause for alarm, which led Dusty to believe the man expected to be either released or in some other way saved from meeting the well-deserved fate of any whiskey peddler who made Indians his customers. Still unable to learn anything from Bristow, Dusty accompanied General Handiman to the main gates where Long Walker waited.

"Well, Chief?" asked Handiman, tossing aside any diplomatic advantage he might have gained by waiting for Long Walker to speak first.

"It is bad and becomes worse," Long Walker admitted frankly. "Many voices spoke to leave this place."

"And will you?"

"Not yet, General. We read the tracks and know that Magic Hands spoke true words for why the three men died. So we will wait to see what you do to the one who sold the whiskey before we decide."

"Does that mean all the bands?" Dusty asked.

"All but the Kweharehnuh are agreed," Long Walker replied. "Their old man chiefs have gone back to speak with the braves and then they will decide."

"Then we can only wait."

"Wait, but hope that nothing else happens, Magic Hands," Long Walker said. "It will take only a small thing to cause the other bands to leave without signing the treaty."

After Long Walker had turned to walk back to his village, Handiman looked at Dusty and gave a long sigh.

"Let's hope that Mr. Manners and the Kid reached the

lancers in time. If Przewlocki jumps that Waw'ai village, this council's wrecked for sure."

Dusty nodded, but his concern was less for the Waw'ai than the lancers.

CHAPTER TWELVE

A TRAIL WITH ONLY ONE END

Night came and a very sober party gathered in the officers' club. Little conversation passed among the members of the committee and the officers seemed affected by the general air of tension. So far, however, the officers showed little outward interest in the treaty council. Most of them knew enough about Indian warfare to want peace, and the general opinion around the fort laid the blame for the trouble with the Kweharehnuh at the right source, upon the whiskey peddler. Only a very few people knew of Colonel Huckfield's death, for Handiman sent word to the colonel's escort to return with his body to his command. Nor had news of the killing of the Reverend Boardwell leaked out.

For all that Dusty knew they balanced on a knife's edge. After a desultory game of poker with Mark, Goodnight, and Houston, Dusty decided to go to bed. Even the officers appeared to be affected by the general feeling and soon everybody turned in.

Dusty was wakened by a knock at the door, then the entrance of a soldier carrying a lantern.

"General Handiman's compliments, Cap'n Fog," the soldier said. "Will you go to the main gate with him?"

"What's up?" Dusty asked, swinging his legs from the bed and reaching for his clothes. A glance out of the window showed him that dawn had not yet broken, although it would soon.

"That Comanche chief come and asked to see the general's all I know," the soldier answered.

Swiftly Dusty and Mark dressed and pulled on their boots. Swinging their gun belts on they followed the soldier and joined Handiman outside the building. The general could not make a guess at what had brought Long Walker to see him at that hour; and he wasted no time trying.

On reaching the gate they found Long Walker standing waiting. Despite the early hour the chief still wore his war-bonnet and a blanket trailed around his shoulders.

"You said for us to send for you any time the chief here wanted to see you, General, sir," the sergeant of the guard reminded Handiman.

"You did the right thing, Sergeant," the general replied. "Greetings, Long Walker. I hope you bring good news."

"The Kweharehnuh have decided," Long Walker answered. "They are leaving."

"You mean at dawn?" Handiman asked.

"They are going now."

"But the treaty—?"

"They decided not to stay and said there is bad medicine here for them."

"Because of the men we had to kill?" said Dusty bitterly.

"The dead must be mourned, Magic Hands," Long Walker replied. "Yet it is in my mind that the Kweharehnuh would have found some other reason to leave."

"They didn't want peace?" Handiman inquired, sounding startled.

"They did not care whether it was made or not," admitted Long Walker.

"Then why did they come here?" the general demanded.

"To see what the white man had to offer and learn how the other bands felt. I have known for many days that the

Kweharehnuh thought of going back to the Palo Duro country and hoped to change their minds. The death of the three *tehnap* gave them their chance to leave."

"How will the rest of the chiefs act now?" Handiman wanted to know.

"They are still willing to listen to your words. I pointed out that none of our bands lived in the Palo Duro country with the Kweharehnuh."

A grin came to Dusty's lips, although he never could remember feeling less like grinning. Of all the Comanche bands the Kweharehnuh lived in the most inaccessible area and the one which the Army would find hardest to operate in. Reminding the other chiefs of that point had been a stroke worthy of a trained diplomat. More than ever Dusty found himself respecting the Kid's grandfather.

"Is all well, then?" asked Handiman, having also taken the point.

"Not yet. I learned this evening that some of the Waw'ai old ones have been saying there would be a fight between their braves and the white lance carriers."

"What's that?" barked the general.

"They said one of their *tsukups* had a dream and saw it. Some of the *tuivitsi* from the different bands rode out last night to see if the dream was true or false."

"Didn't you know about it before?"

"No, General, they did not come to the Pehnane," answered the chief, then looked off into the darkness. "Riders are coming."

Not for several seconds could any white men hear the sound of approaching hooves. Two shapes loomed up, coming out of the growing light, and a chill of apprehension ran through Dusty as he recognized one of them.

"It's Lon," he said. "And Manners."

"They could have come back ahead of the lancers," Handiman answered, trying to sound convincing.

"See the Kweharehnuh're pulling out," the Kid said as he halted his lathered and leg-weary horse.

"Three of their bucks took on a load of whiskey," Dusty explained. "Mark and I had to kill them."

"Is that all?" drawled the Kid, sounding relieved. "I thought that they'd already heard about the lancers."

"What about the lancers?" demanded Handiman, glaring first at the Kid then toward Manners.

"They were wiped out, sir," Manners replied, stiffening his tired frame into a brace. "We failed to reach them in time."

"Which same wasn't Farley's fault," the Kid stated calmly. "The lancers'd got too much of a start on us. Sure, we could've rode all night, but they'd still have pulled out of their camp afore we reached them in the morning and our hosses'd've been too tired to catch up. And those lancers hadn't reached the Waw'ai camp when Sidewinder jumped them."

"You'd best tell me all about it," Handiman said.

"Not here, General," Dusty put in, nodding to where the sentry stood by the gate and the sergeant of the guard hovered in the background. "The less who know about it the better for all concerned."

"If I could offer my tepee, General," Long Walker suggested. "There will be none to hear your words there."

"It could be for the best," Dusty drawled.

"I'll accept your offer then, chief," Handiman replied. "And my thanks."

After telling the sergeant of the guard that he would be accompanying the chief, Handiman walked with the other men to the Pehnane village. Before leaving the gates Manners handed his horse over to the sergeant and asked for it to be cared for. On reaching the tepee, Long Walker told his *pairaivo* that they would be busy and must not be disturbed, then gave some other instructions. Already dressed, the woman nodded and left, crossing to the fire and building it up.

"What happened, Mr. Manners?" asked Handiman, squatting on his heels in an effort to be as comfortable as the Texans and lieutenant.

Manners told his story, speaking slowly and obviously marshaling every fact before passing it on. Clearly he did not want to miss out any detail that might be of use and gave a graphic description of the fight, expressing his wonder again at the Comanches' obvious mastery of the caracole. Yet all the time he spoke, Manners felt conscious that some officer might claim he had acted wrongly in not going to help the lancers.

"I came straight back with the news, sir," he finished, not mentioning a chase by the Kiowa, which only ended when the Kid's deadly Winchester cut down the two leaders after almost a mile. After that the remainder of the party turned their horses and rode back to join the Waw'ai in Wide Valley.

"Which same, we figured that you'd sooner have the news from us than let Sidewinder come whooping in with it," drawled the Kid. "And we couldn't've done more than got killed off happen we'd tried to help the lancers."

"You acted correctly, Mr. Manners," Handiman judged. "And I'll enter it in your record to that effect."

"Thank you, sir," Manners replied, sounding relieved.

"What're you aiming to do about the Waw'ai, General?" Dusty asked. "You'll for sure have to do something."

"Happen you want to keep the peace, you'll have to whale the tar out of those damned Waw'ai, General," Mark went on. "And do it fast."

"I know," Handiman answered. "What force did Sidewinder have along?"

"A hundred men at least, sir. Maybe a hundred and twenty."

"That's close enough," confirmed the Kid.

"How few men can I risk sending?" Handiman mused, speaking half to himself. "If I send too few, it'll be murder.

But if I send out too many I give Sidewinder a boost, make him important. A battalion would be about right."

"Thirty men could handle it," said the Kid. "Happen they took repeaters along and handled things right."

"Explain that a bit further, Kid," requested Handiman.

"Fight 'em Comanche style. Lick them at their own game," the Kid replied. "You'll need your best horsemen, fellers who can live and ride like Indians. And a man who thinks Comanche to ride scout for them."

"Who have you in mind?" Handiman asked.

"Farley Manners here to lead the soldiers," said the Kid. "I'll tend to the rest of it."

"Thirty men?"

"Enough for the way I aim to handle things, General."

"With the Gatling gun, or cannon?"

"They'd slow us up. General, we'll have to ride fifty to a hundred miles a day, live off what we can hunt, and if we don't have any luck go it on berries, roots, leaves. That's the only way we can lick Sidewinder without using so many troops you'll set him up as the big hero of the Nemenuh."

"And you think you can bring the Waw'ai in?" asked Handiman.

"Some of 'em, likely," answered the Kid. "Not Sidewinder, though. When me and him meet, it can have only one end. I crippled him, General, when we was kids. I should've killed him then. If I had, this whole drinking mess'd've never come off. So when I meet up with him, I don't aim to make the same mistake again."

Silence dropped on the tepee and the men looked with interest at the Indian-dark, cowhand-dressed Texan before them. Only, they did not see the Ysabel Kid; instead, they faced a full-blooded Comanche warrior, the most dangerous fighting man ever to draw breath.

"I'll see Colonel Sutter and make the arrangements," Handiman told the others. "Thirty men—?"

"With repeating rifles," agreed the Kid. "The best

hosses the fort can give them. Even if that means taking some officer's pet buffalo-running mount."

"Why not take along two horses each, ride relay?" asked Manners.

"If you've got men who can do it," agreed the Kid.

"You could use one of the horses to carry food and grain for the other," Handiman went on.

"You're still fighting white men, General," the Kid told him. "Those Waw'ai might go for marrying their sisters, and aren't the best fighting men you'll ever meet. But they're Nemenuh, and you'll never lick a Comanche unless you fight him like one."

"All right, Kid," Handiman said. "Play it your way. Mr. Manners, do you know the men you want?"

"I reckon so, sir," Manners replied. "My own troop. I know them and they know me. If I have to, sir, I'll take others. But I'd rather have my own men."

"The choice's yours, mister," Handiman stated. "Now to see the colonel."

"My wife has brought food for Cuchilo and the soldier," Long Walker put in, nodding to the tepee's door. "They have ridden hard all day and need a meal."

"Have it, Mr. Manners," ordered the general.

Any doubts that Manners might have felt at eating with Indians died away when Long Walker's *pairaivo* carried in dishes of steaming stew. He did not care to inquire too closely into the contents of the stew, but had no cause for alarm. The Kid's grandmother knew how to cook white man's fashion and also to add such Indian ingredients as would improve the taste without offending a white's stomach.

With a good meal inside him Manners threw off his tiredness and accompanied Handiman to the fort. Colonel Sutter moved fast on hearing the news. Beyond a few comments on the stupidity of reviving lancers, he ignored the fate of Przewlocki's command. Quickly he set about organizing the gathering of the Kid's requirements.

Without disclosing the reason Sutter arranged for the pick of the fort's remounts to be put at Manners's disposal and gathered his regiment's Spencer carbines in. Although the Spencer had proved its worth during the war, much high-level opposition prevented it from replacing the single-shot Springfield as a general-issue cavalry arm. In times of peace Congress objected to spending money on the more costly repeating arms when the Springfield served the same purpose; and willingly accepted the theory put out by conservative staff officers—secure in desk jobs far from the reach of hostile Indians—that such newfangled weapons only encouraged the soldier to waste ammunition. However, every regiment held a few Spencers on charge for special duties. By calling in all his command's stock, including three privately owned guns, Sutter equipped twenty-five of Manners's party with firearms vastly superior to the one-shot carbines.

At the Pehnane camp the Kid and Long Walker interviewed one of the Waw'ai old men. At first the *tsukup* tended to be arrogant and uncooperative but Raccoon Talker, called from her bed, changed all that. Once assured of Raccoon Talker's medicine protection, and having been made aware of the consequences of refusal, the *tsukup* talked with some considerable willingness on a number of subjects.

Dusty and Mark had been sent from the tepee before the interview began, for no white man could be present when a medicine woman of the Nemenuh exercised her *puha*. Once the old man had hobbled away, to be kept a well-cared-for prisoner until he could do no harm, the two Texans were allowed back into the tepee. On entering they found the Kid stripping off his white man's clothing.

"That damned Fire Dancer's behind this, working hand in glove with those white jaspers who're trying to bust up the treaty," the Kid told his friends as he dropped his clothing onto the bed. "She put the death curse on every *tsukup* and *pu'ste* who wanted to make peace and they all died of it. Got the rest so darned scared, they don't make a move against her."

"Did you learn who the white men are?" asked Dusty.

"He only knows one. A half-breed scout from the fort here. I'm going to have me a talk with him. The *tsukup* described him. Fact being, I may not be able to. The feller he described'd be awful like that scout with the lancers. Only, Sidewinder killed him."

"Why'd he kill off a man who worked with him?" Mark put in.

"You've got me there," drawled the Kid. "Just pure ornery meanness, maybe."

"Or maybe Sidewinder knew he didn't need the scout anymore," guessed Dusty. "What're you doing, Lon?"

Dusty had a good reason for asking the question. Stripped of every item of white man's clothing the Kid cinched a belt around his naked middle. Several items of Comanche dress lay on the bed and the Kid reached for one before replying:

"Sidewinder knows me and how I dress. Happen he gets word that I'm with the soldiers who're after him, he'll be a damned sight harder to handle than if he reckons it's just another Army scout on his trail."

Some time had elapsed since the Kid last wore a breechclout, but he still retained the knack of donning one. Taking the long, broad strip of traditional blue cloth he stepped astride it and drew it up between his legs, tucking one end through the belt at the front and the other at the rear so as to leave flaps that trailed almost to his knees. Next came the buckskin leggings, secured to the belt, followed by a pair of moccasins and then a plain buckskin shirt. Strapping on his gun belt he looked at his friends and grinned at their expressions. Apart from his white-man's short hair he looked every inch a Comanche warrior. However, Mark had thought up a snag to the deception.

"There aren't many scouts who ride white horses and damn few have one the size of Shadow," the blond giant pointed out.

"I can't make him smaller," admitted the Kid, "but Grandpappy Long Walker and me can do something about his color. That's why I asked you to fetch ole Shadow along while we talked to the *tsukup*."

Watched by the two Texans, Long Walker and the Kid used a powder that stained the big white's coat and turned it into a dark bay. While Dusty and Mark had seen the Kid use much the same method to disguise his horse before, he had always been satisfied to make Shadow look like a paint instead of making an overall covering. Knowing that he was operating against a Comanche the Kid did not take that kind of chance. He left off his bedroll, retaining only a couple of blankets fastened Indian style, and discarded his rope; but he kept the saddle boot in which to carry his rifle. Nor did the Texas range saddle strike a false note. Except when hunting buffalo the Comanche always used a saddle, and many obtained Texas rigs through trading or as loot in a raid.

By noon everything had been made ready. Manners's troop, conscious that something out of the ordinary must be afoot, sat their horses and glanced to where the lieutenant stood at General Handiman's side.

"Good luck, Manners," Handiman said. "We can only give you a week at the outside. If you haven't caught up with and licked Sidewinder by then, it will be too late."

"We'll make a try at it, sir," Manners promised.

"I know that," Handiman assured him.

"How about burying the lancers, sir?"

"I'll attend to that. Your business is to nail Sidewinder's hide to the wall as quickly as you can."

On leaving the fort Manners found the Kid waiting and needed to look twice before he recognized the other. In

CHAPTER THIRTEEN

A DEBT REPAID

"I'm going ahead to scout the camp," the Kid told Manners as they halted in the darkness. "Hold your boys here and keep 'em quiet."

"I'll do that."

"*Real* quiet," the Kid emphasized. "If they want to talk, cough, spit, or smoke, stop them. One sound, or a smell of tobacco, and the Waw'ai'll be up and running."

"They'll keep quiet," promised Manners's sergeant, a grizzled veteran called O'Neil. "If they need to."

Something in O'Neil's voice drew the Kid's eyes to him. Suddenly the Kid realized that apart from himself none of the party even knew where the camp was located. If it came to a point, the men did not know the Kid's identity or how come a stranger rode as their scout.

"You'd best come with me, Sergeant," suggested the Kid.

"Go ahead, Sergeant," confirmed Manners, knowing what prompted the Kid's request. "I'll hold the men here."

"Watch Shadow," drawled the Kid as he slipped from the saddle and made his preparations. "Happen he starts moving, follow him and he'll bring you to me."

Taking a strip of meat from the small bundle he carried, the Kid shoved it under his gun belt so that it hung suspended. Then he slung the quiver of arrows across his back, picked up the bow, and nodded to O'Neil. Followed by the sergeant the Kid faded into the darkness.

Before they had covered many yards, the Kid knew he could rely on O'Neil and that the sergeant could move in sufficient silence for their purpose. Side by side they passed over the bush-dotted range. A quarter of a mile fell behind them and the Kid could sense O'Neil's uneasiness growing. Then, as they moved up a slope, both heard a low clatter as if somebody had dropped a cooking pot. Instantly they froze and waited for a time before the Kid gave the order to move on; which he did with a signal.

Flattening to the ground they cautiously peered over the rim and O'Neil expended a considerable amount of willpower in not allowing his surprise to show. At the foot of the slope stood the Waw'ai village, its fires so masked by the tepees that no sight of them had showed to expose their presence. By the central fire a number of young women stood or sat listening to a well-dressed female talking.

"Not many men around," whispered O'Neil.

"Hoss herd and camp guard at most," the Kid agreed. "I'm going down to take a closer look and listen to what that old witch's saying."

"I'd best stay here and cover you."

"Don't start shooting unless you've no other choice," warned the Kid, and drifted over the rim with all the fluid, soundless ease of a stalking cougar.

Making hardly more noise than a shadow the Kid moved down toward the village. His eyes went to Sidewinder's tepee, recognizing it by its central position and from the glow of a lantern inside. None of the other tepees possessed such a sign of affluence and the Kid doubted if Sidewinder would permit any of his braves to outstrip him in such a manner.

A low growl came to the Kid's ears and he saw one of the large, half-starved cur dogs to be found around any

Indian village studying him. Ignoring the bow and arrows the Kid slid the meat from under his belt. He did not wish to kill the dog, for that would mean removing its body, even if he ended its life in silence. While alert, the dog held its warning down to a growl. It caught a mingled smell which confused it; that of Comanche mixed with white man. Before the dog reached any conclusion, the Kid tossed his chunk of meat between its jaws. Instantly the growl died away. Living a scavenger's existence the dog did not aim to pass up good food, and it withdrew without further noise.

Moving on, the Kid reached the rear of Sidewinder's tepee and stood in the darkness. Fire Dancer held out on the subject of good times ahead when the men returned from their raiding mission. Already the Waw'ai brave-hearts had defeated the white lance-carriers, and without loss to themselves, although many coups had been counted. Further success awaited them, and the women must wait until the victorious warriors returned.

Just as the Kid thought of withdrawing, he changed his mind. Maybe he could find some evidence to lead to the white man backing Fire Dancer if he entered the tepee. Not very likely, but worth a try. Quickly he laid aside the bow and quiver, then drew his knife. He did not slash down the side of the tepee, for that would warn Fire Dancer of his visit. Instead he cut across parallel to the ground and eased his way underneath, raising the inner "dew cloth" (the lining of skins that hung down inside the support poles and could be tucked under the beds to prevent any drafts getting in to the sleepers).

The interior of the tepee looked little different from any ordinary dwelling, apart from the hanging lantern. On one bed a *nat'sakena* and *tunawaws,* both empty, along with the lack of weapons, told that the man of the tepee was riding on a war trail or attending to some other business that called for armament and his best clothing, including the war bonnet. As the Kid looked around, he saw a half-consumed *awyaw:t* of pemmican hanging suspended from the poles and a stone jug of honey on the floor. He had paid no attention to them, going instead to the buckskin-decorated medicine bag that rested on the second bed. If the tepee held anything incriminating, that bag would be its hiding place. No Comanche would dare touch a medicine woman as potent as Fire Dancer's property unless possessed of exceptionally strong *puha*. The Kid did not share the general fear and opened the bag. Inside he found the usual items, with one exception; powders, herbs, divining bones, the normal property of a medicine woman—except for the *awyaw:t* of pemmican. Prized item of food that pemmican might be, no woman would think of hiding it in the sacred confines of her medicine bag.

Unless—

Memory stirred and the Kid recalled an almost forgotten incident of his childhood. It stuck out in his mind because on the night in question he killed his first enemy. There had been a victory dance to celebrate the return of a successful raiding party and Fire Dancer was just back from her stay among the Kweharehnuh. One of the Antelope braves who escorted the woman back to the Pehnane died mysteriously that night and his brother blamed the Kid's father. Waiting for Ysabel in a tepee, the brother met the Kid instead and only luck saved the boy. Sam Ysabel always claimed that Fire Dancer tried to poison him; which had been true, although he never proved his suspicions. Looking at the *awyaw:t*, the Kid could guess what had happened. In some way Fire Dancer persuaded the Antelope brave to take a gift of pemmican to Ysabel, but the buck sampled it and for some reason did not deliver the rest. The Kid would never know that the brave had delivered the *awyaw:t*, throwing it into the empty tepee from where a dog stole it.

Cold anger filled the Kid as he thought of the number of people Fire Dancer had caused to die. The two Antelope braves; the Kid's two boyhood friends and her helpers in the attempt at stealing his horse; four husbands most likely went under the same way; not to mention the opposition among the Waw'ai, old men and women who wanted to make peace and found death instead.

Hefting the *awyaw:t* the Kid looked around until his eyes came to rest on the pemmican hanging from the tepee pole. A thought ran through his head and he moved forward to put it into operation. This was not the Ysabel Kid who laughed, joked, and lived as a white man. Instead he had become Cuchilo, grandson of Long Walker, a Pehnane *tehnap* pure and simple.

Taking down the pemmican the Kid carved the second *awyaw:t* until it matched the first. Then he hung up the one from the medicine bag and looked about him to make sure he had left no sign of his presence. With the medicine bag closed and the first *awyaw:t* in his hands, the Kid carefully eased himself over the dew cloth, replaced it, and slid through the slit. More of the curs hovered around and he tossed slices of pemmican to them. Then he took up the bow and quiver, moving off through the darkness in the way he had come.

Although Sergeant O'Neil remained alert, the Kid handed him a shock by materializing at his side.

"The men're all off on a raid," the Kid said. "Only women and a small guard there. We'd best get back to the troop."

"You took a fair time to learn that," O'Neil answered.

"Sure," agreed the Kid. "I stopped off to pay an old debt."

After spending a time calming the fears of the other women, Fire Dancer returned to her tepee. She was about to go to bed when pangs of hunger bit at her and she rose. Taking down the *awyaw:t* of pemmican she carved off a slice and smeared it with honey. Not a single suspicion entered her head as she sat on the bed and began to eat. To the best of her knowledge nobody knew about the poisoned *awyaw:t* in her medicine bag and she knew that no member of the Waw'ai band dare interfere with her property. With honey masking it not even the slightest trace of the poisonous additions to the pemmican came through to give a warning. After eating well Fire Dancer settled down and went to sleep.

"Well?" asked Manners as the Kid and O'Neil returned.

"There're only a handful of braves taking care of things," the Kid replied. "Sidewinder's took the rest out on a raid."

"We can go in and—" O'Neil began.

"Catch us a few gals, maybe Fire Dancer," the Kid finished for him. "And somebody'd be sure to get away, then Sidewinder'll know we're after him already."

"What do we do, then?" Manners said.

"Pull off and go right round the village. We want braves, not gals. I'd bet that Sidewinder's taken the men off in the opposite direction to Wide Valley. He'll know that by now word's reached the fort about the lancers and'll expect that Wide Valley range to be swarming with soldiers."

"But he's gone out to fight," Manners pointed out.

"To raid, not to fight," corrected the Kid. "Sidewinder's no fool. He knows that when he jumps his next bunch of soldiers, they'll be a whole heap harder to handle than the lancers. So he'll steer clear of them and look for some easier way to count coup."

"The soldiers will find his village," O'Neil said.

"They'll try," admitted the Kid. "Comes daylight there'll be scouts out all round the village so that no bunch of soldiers can get near without being seen. Once they're seen, that village can be down and moving faster than any man can trail it. Where'd Sidewinder find the easiest pickings, do you reckon?"

"Something he can hit without too much risk?" asked Manners.

"That's about the size of it."

"Anywhere around here. There're small ranches dotted about everywhere."

"With the lieutenant's permission," O'Neil put in, "I'd suggest down to the south. There're more spreads that way and the stage trail runs through."

"And it's in almost the opposite direction to Wide Valley," agreed Manners. "That's the way we'll go then."

When safely clear of the circle of Waw'ai village guards, the troop halted for the night. Instead of following normal soldier practice, making fires and cooking up food, they ate hardtack and jerked meat in the darkness and slept wrapped in blankets, huddled together for added warmth. At dawn they moved on, going south with every eye raking the country ahead for the first sign of the enemy's tracks.

"Nothing!" said the Kid disgustedly.

"This's a big country," Manners answered. "Their tracks could be running parallel to our line over the next rim."

"Only, they don't!" the Kid growled and pointed.

A column of smoke rose into the air on the horizon, growing larger by the second. One thought came to each man's mind as he recalled other times he had seen similar smoke. Only blazing hay built up such a volume of smoke so quickly, and hay meant a ranch. Manners did not waste time in idle chatter.

"Troop forward by twos!" he barked. "Yo!"

Despite his eagerness to reach the column of smoke, Manners held the pace of his troop down to a level that wasted no time but still retained a reserve of speed should it prove necessary. Two hours almost elapsed before the men came into sight of the fire. By that time it had burned itself out, the barn being only smoking ruins, although the small house still stood untouched. No horses remained in the corral and two men's scalped, mutilated bodies lay by its ruined fence. As the soldiers rode up, a yell greeted them and a scared-looking cowhand limped from the house. While wounded in the leg, he was still alive; a fact which appeared to be as surprising to him as to the newcomers.

"They didn't kill me!" the man gasped. "Had me dead to rights as I crawled into the house and let me get the door closed. They could've still got me had they tried, but they just took all they wanted and rode off."

"See to the man's wound, one of you," ordered Manners.

"Leave one of the men without a repeater to tend to him, Farley," the Kid put in. "We've got to ride."

Normally a troop of soldiers who came on such an incident would stay to bury the dead and do what they could to clean up the mess. The wounded man showed signs of surprise when Manners clearly did not intend to do so. However, Manners saw the Kid's point. While they wasted time, Sidewinder would be getting farther and farther away. Even as the troop, less one man, prepared to leave, they saw more smoke rising in the distance.

"That's the Villiers' place!" gasped the cowhand. "Hell! He's married and got a little gal."

"Move out!" Manners snapped, and the troop set off again.

Six miles later the Kid, ranging ahead of the others, came into sight of the Villiers ranch. However, the Comanche had departed, taking every horse from the corrals and doing damage. Once again they had not fired the house. Villiers had been lucky. Seeing the Waw'ai approaching, he had shown commendable speed of thought in taking his family and cowhands into the house, from where they held off the attack, even though unable to prevent the loss of their horses and some damage. Naturally Villiers expressed himself strongly on the subject of Indians, when the soldiers arrived, and damned the idea of making peace with the Comanches.

The Kid sat silent and did not attempt to explain the difference between the Comanche at the peace council and Sidewinder's bunch of bad-hat bucks. In the interests of diplomacy Manners kept quiet also and told the rancher that the troop must move on if they hoped to catch up with the attackers and perhaps recover the stolen horses.

"There's a pattern to it," the Kid said as he led Manners along the Waw'ai's trail. "They're leaving somebody alive each time to spread the story."

"Sidewinder could just be trying to count coup and gather loot without taking chances," Manners objected.

"After whipping the lancers he wouldn't need to show his medicine's power," the Kid drawled. "Had they wanted to get him, that wounded cowhand couldn't've stopped them. And they'd've stuck to Villiers' place longer if they'd aimed to take him."

Shortly before noon they once more saw smoke drifting into the air. Manners gave a low growl, for his men had pushed their horses at a good speed and yet the Waw'ai still retained a lead as great as when they first started out that morning to investigate the original attack.

"Damn it," he said. "They'll be gone before we reach that ranch."

"Sure," the Kid agreed. "We've got to catch up with 'em, not trail along behind, following their smoke."

"What do you suggest?"

"They've been swinging to the west all the while. Likely they aim to make a complete circle and pick up the womenfolk on the way back, then high-tail it for the open range."

"So?"

"So happen we can reach some place to the west of that burning spread, we might catch them there, or even beat them to it."

"Let's take a look at the map while the horses rest."

Studying the map he had brought along, Manners followed a line in a rough circle from the first attacked ranch. He tapped his finger on the next spread's home buildings and remarked that it would take some riding to reach the place in time.

"Then let's leave it," the Kid replied. "This's where I'd say we go."

Looking at the spot the Kid's finger touched, Manners shook his head. "It's well beyond the ranch—"

"But it's a Wells Fargo relay station," answered the Kid. "And you know what that means. Hosses."

"Yes," agreed Manners, sounding puzzled.

"Those bucks with Sidewinder aren't along for a ride or sport. They want loot and hosses most of all. So he'll take them where they can get their wantings."

"They might hit at that ranch—"

"We still won't be there soon enough to stop them, or help out."

"All right, then. We go your way."

"Reckon I'll scout ahead and see what's happening," the Kid said as the men rode across the range in the direction of the relay station.

"We'll keep moving as fast as we can," Manners replied.

Urging his horse forward at a faster pace the Kid soon disappeared over the horizon. Once clear of the others he employed all his skill to travel fast and avoid allowing himself to be conspicuous. Tirelessly the big white loped on, its iron-hard condition enabling it to outdistance the soldiers. Yet the Kid knew he could rely on Shadow to gallop at high speed if needed.

The sun began its downward dip toward the western horizon and the Kid rode through bush-dotted range country about a mile ahead of the soldiers. Slowing the big stallion he studied a metallic glinting and then took cover. In a short time he saw the cause of the glinting. Two Waw'ai bucks rode through the bushes some distance away. Up to that moment they had been hidden, but one of them carried a U.S. Army lance over his shoulder and its tip rose high enough to top the bushes. Dropping from his horse the Kid studied the Waw'ais and decided they must be either scouts, or two bucks who had decided to strike out on their own. In either case they had to be stopped, for the route they traveled would take them into sight of the soldiers. One sight of the troop would send the two bucks racing back to Sidewinder and warn him of the danger.

Thinking fast the Kid formed a plan that he felt would meet his needs. He must stop both braves; killing one and allowing the other to escape was no use at all. So he prepared to lay a trap and draw the bucks in. Quickly he stripped the stallion's saddle, blanket, and bridle off and hid them under a bush. Then he let Shadow advance into the open and begin to graze. Not knowing how many more Waw'ai might be in hearing distance, the Kid discarded his rifle and took up the bow instead. With everything ready he moved into cover and waited.

On coming into sight of the big horse the Waw'ai scouts halted and studied it with interest. However, they did not move in straightaway to pick up such a valuable piece of loot. Even with the stain on its coat the stallion looked a magnificent animal, yet it bore the signs of regularly carrying a saddle. If the Kid hoped to have the men ride in close enough for him to deal with them he needed to lull their suspicions and figured he knew just the way to do it.

Loud in the air rang the cackling gobble of a tom turkey, sounding from down close to the horse. The Waw'ais exchanged satisfied glances. No tom turkey would give its call in the presence of its prime enemy, man. Feeling assured that they were running into no danger, the braves advanced.

Crouching hidden among a clump of bushes the Kid watched his plan succeed. When he imitated the turkey's call, he hoped to fool the Waw'ai and had done just that. His eyes took in every detail of the two men's armament and dress. Clearly they had been at Wide Valley, for both wore items of U.S. Cavalry clothing in addition to the lance that had given them away to the Kid. However, he felt less concerned over the lance than the twin-barreled shotgun held by the second brave. That would be the dangerous weapon, its spreading load a menace even in the hands of a poor shot. It looked a mighty fine gun, too, not a cheap trade weapon. Although the Kid did not know it, he was watching the killer of the Reverend Boardwell, recently returned to his people and riding on a loot-gathering raid.

Matched against odds of two to one and with such important issues at stake, the Kid could not play the game in a sporting manner. He allowed the braves to ride by and then rose, bringing up the bow and drawing back its string until the arrow's flight brushed against his ear. Swiftly, yet carefully, he released his hold on the string and the arrow sprang forward. Even as the string twanged against the Kid's wrist and its noise warned the Waw'ai of their danger, the arrow sliced into the second brave's back.

The bushes did not permit the Kid free enough movement, so he lunged through them and into the open as soon as he sank his arrow into the brave. Body contorting in agony, the shotgun clattering to the ground, the Kid's victim slid from his horse without a sound.

Not so the first brave. Bringing his horse around in a fast turn he swung the lance from his shoulder and into the lined position. A lance carrier disdained the use of any other weapon, and the brave intended to live or die by the tradition of the Nemenuh. Shouting his war cry he sent the horse hurling toward the Kid, and the lance in his hands made a more formidable weapon than when its original owner wielded it.

Reaching back over his shoulder the Kid started to draw another arrow. At the same moment he flung himself across the front of the charging horse. In doing so he avoided the lance thrust and put himself in a place where the steel head could not speedily be brought to bear on him. While moving he notched the arrow and was already drawing back on the string as he swung around. With superb skill the Waw'ai swung his horse in a rump-scraping turn and prepared to attack again. Once more the Kid drew his bow and released an arrow. Flying shaft and charging Waw'ai converged. The arrow head, set at right angles to the string notch, passed between the Indian's ribs and into the vital organs beyond. Even so the Kid had to avoid the charge by leaping aside. Death came to the Waw'ai before he could turn or make a further attempt, and his body crashed to the ground.

Instantly the Kid sought cover and lay with an ear to the ground. He did not know how many more braves might be in the vicinity, but the lance carrier's yells might have reached to other ears. However, he could pick up no sounds other than those of the departing mount of the dead lance carrier. Rising, the Kid checked to make sure he did not need to take further action against the two scouts. Then he collected his saddle and went to the waiting stallion.

CHAPTER FOURTEEN

A DISAPPOINTMENT FOR THE YSABEL KID

"They've not reached the relay station yet," the Kid said as he rejoined Manners's troop. "Place's quiet and I didn't go in."

"Traveling at speed they ought to be here," Manners said worriedly.

"They'll likely be going slower now," the Kid drawled. "Don't forget they've a fair bunch of stolen horses along by now."

"That would slow them down," the lieutenant agreed. "But if we've guessed wrong—"

"I don't reckon we have. Had me a run-in with a couple of scouts who were down this ways."

"Did you kill them?"

"Sure. Figured it was best. Sidewinder won't jump the station today, it's too near nightfall. But he'd send out a couple of bucks to see what was doing. If I hadn't stopped them, they'd've seen you."

"Won't he be suspicious when they don't return?" Manners asked.

"Maybe," answered the Kid. "Most likely, though, he'll figure they've found something worth watching and'll go through with the raid on the station."

"Only, we'll be there waiting for him," Manners said.

"That's just where we'll be," agreed the Kid. "If we handle things right, we'll have him and his bunch whipsawed and end it right here."

"How do we play it?" asked O'Neil.

"Careful," the Kid replied, and went on to explain his plan.

Dawn slowly crept up in the east and the tired men at their posts about the relay station stirred restlessly. They had covered almost seventy miles the previous twenty-four hours, and with little sleep, so the long vigil through the night left them irritated and tense. For all that they remained silent, following the orders given to them by Manners in accordance with the Kid's plan.

By the corral, in their impromptu firing positions, the Kid and ten soldiers scanned the range for the first sight of the enemy. Skilled Indian-fighters all, they knew that the Comanche's favorite attacking time came soon. The Kid gave the surrounding area a quick study and nodded in satisfaction at what he saw. Or rather did not see, for the groups of men in the various buildings remained out of sight.

Suddenly the Waw'ai appeared. Some twenty or so braves rose out of the ground, or so it seemed. Taking advantage of every scrap of cover, unnoticed even by the most keen eyed of the soldiers, the braves drifted down on the silent station.

A rifle cracked from the barn where one of the soldiers had been dropping to sleep, fighting it off as best he could, and shook himself awake in time to see the Waw'ai advancing. Pure instinct caused him to press his Spencer's trigger and ruin the Kid's plan. Before any human agency could have stopped it, every soldier fired his carbine. The shots came in a rippling, jagged roll rather than the smooth crash of a volley, and lead tore into the Indians. Caught in a murderous crossfire nine of the braves went down and at least three more caught minor wounds. Not a bad result if they had formed the entire party. Turning, the remainder of the Waw'ai went bounding back in the direction from which they had come.

"We did 'em!" whopped one of the men with the Kid and started to rise.

Even as the Kid opened his mouth to growl a warning, a rifle cracked from in the bushes toward which the disrupted party fled. The soldier gave a little cough, staggered, spun around, and fell to the ground. Next moment hooves thundered and the main body of the Waw'ai burst into view and charged down at the station.

Stiffened with cold the soldiers' hands fumbled at recharging their carbines. Down swung the loading levers, ejecting empty cartridge cases and then lifting to slide a loaded bullet into the chamber. After that the side hammer must be drawn back; the detail prevented the .50 caliber carbine from ever attaining a speed of fire equal to the Winchester. For all that the Spencer could be fired far faster than the single-shot trapdoor Springfields issued to the majority of the cavalry. A second ragged volley ripped into the Indians, bringing down several men and horses. While the soldiers still went through their reloading sequence, the remainder of the Waw'ai spun their horses around, scooped up dead or wounded companions, and withdrew. Instead of descending on an unprepared relay station to gather easy loot and coups, they had stirred up a hornet's nest of opposition.

Angrily the Kid lowered his rifle. He alone of the defenders had not fired any shots. While the attackers charged, he searched their ranks for a sign of Sidewinder. A bullet through the chief's head would halt the attack and cause a hurried departure of the rest of the band. However, Sidewinder did not appear to be among those present. Clearly he allowed his position as a namewarrior to give him the right to keep back while others did the fighting. A magnanimous gesture in Comanche eyes, as it permitted those less fortunate in the matter of gathering coups to collect a greater share of the glory. Being a warbonnet chief Sidewinder no longer needed to enhance his fame.

"That's done 'em!" enthused one of the Kid's party.

"They'll be back," replied the Kid. "How is he?"

"Dead," answered the soldier who knelt by the shot man.

"Six of you get through the corral and watch the back," the Kid ordered. "We've got to hold on here until hell freezes."

Should the Waw'ai manage to drive off the horses, they would leave Manners's patrol with no means of continuing the pursuit when they withdrew. So the Kid had the largest group of men accompanying him in the defense of the corral. Six more held the blacksmith's forge, eight defended the barn, and the rest, under Manners, guarded the main building. However, each group covered the others and gave support against a frontal attack.

Having seen the result of one frontal attack, Sidewinder did not intent to make another. Sitting his horse in a sheltered, but commanding, position, the chief studied the situation and formed his conclusions. The dead soldier by the corral, taken with the spirited opposition to his men, told that an Army patrol was defending the relay station. Not a large patrol, Sidewinder concluded as he examined the horses in the big corral. A man skilled in such matters could tell the difference between saddlehorses and the heavier, strong animals used to haul Wells Fargo stagecoaches. By counting the number of horses used for riding, Sidewinder drew his conclusions and acted on them. From the position of the defenders he knew the soldiers were split up in small groups. Yet he also saw their strength and knew he could accomplish nothing while all four positions remained in his enemies' hands.

Calling his junior leaders to him Sidewinder gave orders. He had well over a hundred and twenty-five men at his back now, even after the losses of the thwarted attack due to small bands of restless young *tuivitsi* having joined him. Numerical odds favored the Waw'ai and their tactics must be tailored to fit the occasion. Swinging away the young leaders went to put their chief's plans into operation.

Telling the men at the front of the corral to keep their eyes open, the Kid slipped back, rose, and darted through the milling horses. Before he reached the rear, he heard a couple of shots and the drumming of hooves. As he arrived, the Kid saw a small bunch of Waw'ai charging through the bushes while the defenders fired at them. The whiplike crack of the Winchester mingled with the deeper boom of the Spencers and a brave slid sideways from his horse. Then the attackers turned and withdrew, darting out of sight like scared whitetail deer.

"Stop that shooting!" barked the Kid as the soldiers fired after the departing Waw'ai without scoring any hits.

Although each man carried one of the special ammunition boxes, which held ten copper tubes containing seven bundles each—to facilitate rapid recharging of magazines—they had no other source of supply and must not be allowed to waste bullets.

"They're not pushing home their attacks," one of the soldiers commented.

"Would you?" said the Kid dryly. "I sure hope those fellers in the other places watch their backs."

Before sending the men to their positions the Kid had lectured them on Comanche tactics and hoped that his warning had sunk in. Rising, he once more crossed the corral and heard the crackle of shots from the main building. He reached the front of the corral in time to check the men there and prevent them from wasting bullets by firing at the fast-riding attackers who struck at the flank of the blacksmith's shop. Any objections the soldiers might have felt at not being allowed to help their comrades died as they saw the Waw'ai pull back.

For a time the Waw'ai made darting rushes that halted before coming in too close, yet kept the defenders on the alert, drew fire, and wasted Army bullets with little effect.

Once in a while an Indian would be hit, but not often enough to repay the number of bullets used and which failed to strike home. Manners saw that and took advantage of a lull in the rushes to yell a warning.

"Hold down the shooting, Sergeant O'Neil!" he yelled. "Make sure you're going to hit something afore you throw lead."

"Yo!" came O'Neil's reply from the barn.

"You hear me, Corporal Saggers?" Manners continued.

"Yo!" answered the noncom in command of the party in the forge.

However, it seemed that the Waw'ai had given up their tactics, for no more rushes came. Time dragged by and the Kid searched the range anxiously. After such a string of victories it hardly seemed likely that Sidewinder's men would give up so easily. By now there would be deaths to avenge and each brave had the inducement of obtaining repeating carbines should they overrun the soldiers defending the station. No, sir, the Kid knew they were far from being out of the wood.

Then it happened!

Down swarmed by far the largest body of Waw'ai horsemen so far seen at one time. The ground shook under the thunder of hooves and the massed bunch headed for the main building. To do so they must run through the horseshoe curve formed by the barn, forge, and corral. Having been heavily overgrazed and constantly worn at by countless wheels and hooves, the immediate area surrounding the station held only a sparse coating of grass. The dry earth churned up into rolling clouds of dust under the Waw'ai horses, swirling around the attackers and making them difficult targets. In the main house Manners shot at a blurred shape, saw it slide from its horse—or thought he did, for the horse still carried a rider.

In the face of such a concentrated attack the men at the front of the forge emptied their carbines. After watching the rear for a time the soldiers turned to help their comrades at the front. There had been no sign of attackers at the rear and so the soldiers wanted to throw their weight where it would do most good. O'Neil swung around, meaning to drive the men back to their posts and caught a chance Indian bullet between the shoulders. Left without a leader the soldiers gathered at the front and overlooked the fact that a door and two large windows faced the rear.

Darting forward on foot a dozen or so Waw'ai arrived unseen at the rear of the barn. Some of them came around the outer side and all held firearms of one kind or another. Glass shattered as the braves smashed the windows, then the door burst in. Although the soldiers turned, lead ripped into them. Three men fell with their weapons pointing out of the front, two more died as they tried to turn and fight. Firing at the Waw'ai one of the remaining pair sought cover in a stall. His companion cut down one before a rifle blasted through the window at his back and he fell. For a time the soldier in the stall fought, but his Spencer only held seven bullets fully loaded and he had been using it at the attackers before the building. Sighting at a brave who dived through the window, the soldier heard a hollow click instead of feeling a recoil kick and catching the sound of the exploding powder's roar. Dropping the empty carbine he reached for his Army Colt and a bullet from a Winchester rifle ripped into his head. The barn was now in Waw'ai hands.

Much the same happened at the forge. Being more open than the barn, the men at the rear saw everything that happened and decided that they would be better employed helping at the front instead of watching the rear. To their amazement they suddenly found themselves assaulted from the rear and sides by braves on foot. A savage, bloody little struggle took place in the forge as rifle butts, knives, and even the shoeing hammers were wielded. Up close like that firearms were of no use and soldiers, outnumbered as well as taken by surprise, fought gallantly but with little hope of victory. Two of their number, seeing the others go down, made a dash for the main building. Down swept a brave carrying a U.S. Army lance and its head skewered the nearer soldier. Two bullets struck his companion and he crumpled into the churned-up dirt.

Firing his rifle fast the Kid tumbled the lance carrier just an instant too late to save the soldier. Then he realized what had happened. Yelling to the men around him to carry on, he turned and ran through the horses to the rear. He came in time to find the men preparing to leave their posts so as to help those at the front.

"Watch those bushes!" the Kid roared, his rifle coming up and roaring.

Any doubts the defenders might have felt ended as they saw a Waw'ai buck rear up into sight, spin around, and fall. Then more of the Indians burst into view; only, they were uninjured, armed, and making a determined charge.

"Pour it into 'em!" roared the Kid, right hand blurring the Winchester's loading lever.

Not that he needed to give the order—the men with him saw their danger and acted on it. Shot after shot tore into the charging attackers and the soldiers fired with the carbines rested on the corral fence rails to gain added accuracy. Aiming at an advancing brave the Kid heard the awesome scream of an angry stallion followed by the cry of a man in mortal pain. He squeezed off the shot, saw his man crash to the ground, and swung toward the origin of the scream. While he could see nothing but whirling dust and milling horses, the Kid guessed what had happened. Obviously the Waw'ai were playing the old Comanche trick of coming to the attack with a number of braves riding double and the man at the rear slipping unnoticed, if he could, off the horse at an opportune moment.

One such brave had reached and entered the corral. Unfortunately for him he came across the Kid's big stallion. While Shadow remained peaceable and allowed the soldiers to move by him as long as they kept their distance, the same did not apply to a Waw'ai making a sudden appearance close up when he stunk of hate.

Slipping between the corral rails the Kid darted along the outside. His rifle spat twice, tumbling a charging brave into the dirt. Then he reached a point where he could see the braves of whom Shadow's victim had been one. Seeing the fate of their companion they remained outside the corral and moved around to take the soldiers at the front by surprise.

Flame spurted from the Kid's rifle and its lever moved like a blur. Two of the braves fell, then a third spun around as a bullet caught him. The rest of the small group whirled about to meet the fresh danger and the Kid shot twice more while the nearest soldiers heard their danger and also cut in. Under such a hail of lead the Waw'ai broke and darted away.

When forming his plan Sidewinder counted on the soldiers being armed with the usual Springfield carbines. Instead, his men ran into the rapid-shooting Spencers and broke before the repeated fire. Whirling their horses they retired the way they had come. Scooping up fallen, wounded companions, or men who had ridden up behind companions before fighting on foot, the Indians withdrew.

Not all, though. The braves who had taken the barn and forge remained in their positions and most of them held firearms. A bullet ripped the air over the Kid's head, and he dived into the corral. Swiftly he fed ammunition through the Winchester's loading slot until its magazine was full once more.

"We're in trouble," stated the soldier at the Kid's right side, a grizzled veteran with long experience to guide his summing up of the situation.

"Looks that way," the Kid agreed as a bullet from the forge sent splinters of wood flying. "I don't reckon we can hold out here."

While their position in the corral had been reasonably safe before, the loss of the barn and forge changed all that. Instead of having friends giving covering fire from the two buildings, the Kid's party now found themselves in inadequate shelter and being fired on.

"Looks that way," admitted the soldier.

"Hey, Farley!" yelled the Kid.

"Yes?" came Manners's reply from the house.

"We'll have to come over there and chance losing the hosses. They've got the barn and forge."

"Hold hard until I can organize covering fire."

"Yo!" answered the Kid, and looked at the soldier. "Go bring in the men from the other side."

Even as he spoke, the Kid knew just how little time they had. Already the Waw'ai had formed up once more. Another rush, backed by the men at the forge, would see the corral guard wiped out and the horses freed. Then the Waw'ai could withdraw without loss of face, having gathered up loot and counted coup. Bitter disappointment filled the Kid as he scanned the enemy ranks in the hope of seeing Sidewinder. The chief still did not make an appearance and the Kid cursed. It seemed that he would either die, or be driven into the house, without having a chance to kill his old enemy.

The old soldier brought the other men forward and they lay in what cover they could find. All understood the gravity of the situation and their set faces told the Kid he did not need to emphasize it.

"All right," he said quietly. "As soon as the folks at the house start shooting we'll run. Go like hell—and go shooting."

Before anybody could reply, a Waw'ai let out a wild yell and the whole bunch came racing forward in a rush that sought to crush the Kid's party by sheer weight of numbers.

CHAPTER FIFTEEN

A CHANCE TO MAKE A LASTING PEACE

Something hissed through the air over the Kid's head and exploded above the charging Waw'ai. An instant later a different hissing sounded and he saw a strange, smoke-trailing object curve from behind him to strike the ground ahead of the attackers and erupt in a cloud of flame. Men and horses had gone down under the first midair explosion and the Waw'ai tried to rein their mounts to a halt. Rearing, sliding, emitting screams of fear, the horses slammed into each other and only superb riding kept the Indians astride.

On a rim nine hundred yards away Dusty Fog watched through his borrowed field glasses. To one side of him a soldier slid another Hale spin-stabilized rocket into the launcher, checked his aim, and fired it. Not quite so quick to reload, the mountain howitzer to Dusty's other side bellowed out as the rocket streaked its eerie way through the air. Using spherical case shells, which exploded in midair by means of a time fuse, the howitzer gunner showed his skill. Again his charge exploded right where it did most good, just over the heads of the disrupted Waw'ai. With only a light bursting charge in the case, the shell lacked power, yet its moral effect was great and it did put down a couple of men and a horse or so each time.

Far more effective, for once, proved the rockets. Using an incendiary charge that threw up a sheet of flame on impact, the Hale rocket served to throw the already disrupted Indians into a panic.

"We only just came in time," Dusty said to Mark Counter, who stood at his side. "Here comes the cavalry."

Across to the left of the Waw'ai a troop of cavalry came into sight and launched a charge. After their repulses at the station, followed by the howitzer and rocket bombardment, the Waw'ai needed only to see the arrival of the cavalry to conclude their medicine had gone completely bad. Long before contact could be made with them, they burst into fast-riding fragments, tiny groups of men speeding away at full speed and with only one aim in mind, to save their necks.

At the corral the Kid saw what happened and rose, ducking through the rails. "Come on!" he yelled. "We've got to clear those yahoos out of the barn."

Already the Waw'ai in the barn and forge knew their danger. True to their Comanche upbringing a party of braves tried to bring mounts to their friends. The Kid and his companions risked death to shoot at the riders, for he knew that no greater disgrace could befall a Comanche warrior than to leave living friends to fall into enemy hands.

Although not sure just how the help came to be on hand, Manners wasted no time in leading a rush of men from the main building, charging at the barn—half of the party making for the forge. Faced with such opposition the Waw'ai broke and ran, to be picked off by the soldiers. Not one brave who left either place reached safety and none were taken prisoner. Sidewinder's raid had ended. After such a crushing defeat he would need long days of medicine making before he might hope to induce the braves to follow him.

"Are you all right, Lon?" asked Dusty, having come tearing up on his big paint stallion.

"Sure," the Kid replied, seeing the relief on his two

friends' faces as they dropped from their horses and advanced on him. "You pair came just in time."

"It looked that way," drawled Mark.

"How'd you get here just right?" the Kid inquired.

"That soldier you left with the wounded cowhand used his head," Dusty explained. "The two of them rode double, aiming to reach the fort, and had some luck. They picked up a hoss that's been turned loose to range-graze and made good time. From what the cowhand told us, General Handiman figured you might need some help and we had a talk with Long Walker. It was him who told us where to come. Lord knows how he knew, but he was right."

While Dusty and Mark stood talking with the Kid, soldiers entered the barn or forge. Soon the men came out once more, gathered in a group close to where the Texans stood. Anger showed on each soldier's face, for all had lost friends when the two positions were overrun.

"Them damned Injuns!" one of the soldiers spat out. "And to think we're feeding 'em at the fort and're ready to make peace with 'em."

"I say we ought to go back and hand them the same as they gave our boys," another went on.

"Soldier!" the word cracked from Dusty's lips and drew every eye to him. "It was one of those Indians back at the fort who told us where to find you. Then, so that we could get the howitzer and rockets here, some more of them loaned us their best pack horses. They did it even though they knew it would get some of their people killed. Some of them even guided us out here. We'd never've reached you in time without their help."

"So?" asked the first speaker sullenly.

"So this," Dusty answered. "I don't know what you figure your life's worth. But whatever you figure on it, that's just what you owe to Long Walker and the other Comanche chiefs."

Having been one of the Kid's party at the corral, the

soldier knew just how slight his chance of reaching safety had been. He looked at Dusty, then to Mark and the Kid. Something in the Texans' eyes warned him not to take the matter further, even though he could not see the people Dusty claimed to have helped them.

One of the men from the main building, not appreciating the danger of the corral party, felt less inclined to accept the Texans' words.

"That bunch we've been after for the past two days sure had a strange way of wanting peace," he stated.

"There're good and bad in every race, soldier," Mark replied. "Those Waw'ai didn't want peace. But there're white men who feel the same way. Only, they don't go out and raid, they just supply the Indians with guns and let them do it."

"Why'd they do that?" demanded the soldier.

"To make folks feel like you do now," Dusty explained. "To make them hate all Indians, even the ones who want peace."

While the Texans put a different complexion on the matter, the soldier did not feel entirely assured.

"That bunch didn't want peace," he repeated.

"They will after the mauling you handed them," Dusty answered. "And it was you here at the station who licked 'em. Sure, we helped chase them off. But you men held them here, kept them so busy that they didn't see us coming. It's you who've broken Sidewinder's medicine. His men won't follow him again."

"Which same I never saw Sidewinder," the Kid said bitterly.

Looking across the range he knew that there would be no chance of finding the chief's tracks among the many that left the area. If he had known the tracks of Sidewinder's horse the Kid might have accomplished something. Without that knowledge he could only guess at which fleeing group included the chief. It seemed that once more Ka-Dih favored Sidewinder and allowed the chief to slip through the Kid's hands.

"Hey. Look there!" yelled one of the soldiers, and pointed off across the range.

On turning, Dusty, Mark, and the Kid saw a welcome sight. Colonel Goodnight rode toward them, accompanied by Long Walker, War Club, and four other elderly Comanches, driving a large bunch of riderless horses.

"Those're your Indians who don't want peace," Dusty told the soldier. "Long Walker and War Club, two chiefs of the Pehnane. The others are the chiefs of the Yap Eaters, Liver Eaters, Water Horse, and Burnt Meat bands. They're the ones who told us about the raid"—Dusty felt he could tell a small lie under the circumstances—"and who got us here in time to help you out."

"How'd they know about the raids?" asked the soldiers.

"Likely got the word from a medicine man," the Kid put in. "And don't sell them short, soldier. They know things that no fancy eastern professor can explain."

"No matter how they knew," Mark went on, "they got us here and it looks like they've brought in all the horses the Waw'ai picked up on the raids."

"That won't bring back the folks those other Indians've killed," protested the soldier who had done most of the talking.

"Look around you, soldier!" Dusty ordered. "There are fifty or more dead Waw'ai hereabouts, not counting any the others carried away. Just how many more lives do you want?"

No reply came from the soldiers, and they stood in a silent group. Yet Dusty knew he had given them food for thought. Then Manners came out of the barn, face haggard and body drooping in tiredness. Slowly he walked over to the Texans.

"You did it, Farley?" Dusty said.

"I lost half of my patrol," Manners replied. "Was it worth it?"

"You saw how those Waw'ai could fight," Dusty answered. "And they're not the toughest Comanche band. It's better to have peace with folk who fight that good."

"I'd best start work." Manners sighed, not commenting on Dusty's remark.

"Wait for Captain Connel's troop to help you," Dusty suggested. "They're coming back now."

After following the scattering Waw'ai for a time the second troop of soldiers came back to the relay station. At the same time Goodnight walked over from where he and the Comanche halted the recovered horses.

"Long Walker and the others called it right on where we'd find the Waw'ai stock," he said. "And they sure haven't forgotten how to handle themselves in a raid."

"Did you have any trouble, Uncle Charlie?" asked Dusty.

"Nope. Sidewinder only left four bucks guarding the horses and they never had a chance to make a fight."

"Then we've got all the loot back, except for maybe a few guns."

"Sure, Dusty."

Manners stood with Captain Connel, and the soldiers mingled in talking groups. It seemed that the second troop's members praised the manner in which Long Walker and the other Comanche chiefs had guided them across the range, for some of the hostility died away among the group that had held the relay station.

"I've left men out on the range, gathering the lances that the Waw'ai are discarding, Dusty," Colonel said. "Why'd they take them from Przewlocki's men in the first place, if they aimed to throw them away?"

"Took them to show they'd whipped the white soldier lance carriers," the Kid explained. "And threw them away to save weight on the hosses' backs—and because they figured those lances brought bad luck."

"They could be right at that." Connel grunted. "They sure didn't do Przewlocki's men any good at all. I've told

Farley Manners to rest his men and mine'll start the cleaning up here. Unless you figure on following the Waw'ai up, Dusty."

"How about it, Lon?" asked Dusty.

"You could try," drawled the Kid. "But they'll not gather together again for days and won't stop running until they're back with the rest of the band. I'd bet that the Waw'ai come in after this. Or would if we could get Sidewinder. While he's out, if he can get his medicine back, they'll never settle down."

"Then we'd best try to get him," Dusty said.

"We can try," agreed the Kid doubtfully. "Tell me which set of tracks to follow and I'll make a go at it."

"Maybe he's gone back to the camp aiming to collect his mother," Dusty guessed. "From what you told me about him, he always stuck pretty close to her."

"It's worth trying," the Kid admitted. "Let's get our hosses and go see."

"Is that all right with you, Tom?" Dusty asked, looking at Connel.

"Go to it, Dusty. Do you want any men?"

"We'll handle it ourselves," Dusty replied, glancing at his two friends and Goodnight. "Coming, Uncle Charlie?"

"I figured to take those horses to their owners and make sure that the owners know who got them back," Goodnight replied.

Knowing the respect in which most Texans held Goodnight, Dusty could see that his uncle's decision was the correct one. If anybody could smooth down the hostility caused by Sidewinder's raids, or ensure that it went to the right source, Goodnight stood the best chance of doing it.

"You might run into some of the Waw'ai," Connel warned.

"They'll likely not be wanting to fight anymore," Dusty answered. "But in case they do, we'll ask the chiefs to come with us. Maybe they'll be able to talk any Waw'ai we meet out of fighting."

"Or help us with the fighting if talk doesn't work," drawled Mark.

On having Dusty's suggestion put to them the chiefs agreed with considerable enthusiasm to going along. In fact, judging by the way they fingered their weapons, Dusty reckoned that the chiefs hoped for a meeting if it gave them a chance at one final fight before going on to the reservation to live a boring, peaceful life.

The ride proved uneventful, with no sign of Waw'ai and nothing of interest happening. At noon the following day the men arrived at the site of the village and found that only one tepee remained. Recognizing the tepee, a cold, hard smile twisted the Kid's lips and he could have made a mighty good guess at what lay ahead of them, even before his keen nostrils caught the unmistakable smell of death that came from Sidewinder's home.

Drawing up his bandana over his nose Dusty slipped from the paint and approached the tepee. He lifted the flap and stepped inside, peering through the gloom and not liking what he saw. In the center of the tepee a well-dressed elderly woman's body sprawled twisted and contorted, its face a hideous mask of pain and horror. Close by the body lay a medicine bag, its contents scattered around as if the woman had upended it in an effort to find something that might help her.

"It's Fire Dancer," said the Kid from the tepee door.

"She looks like she's been poisoned," Dusty replied, having twice seen poison victims and knowing the signs.

"Must have been something she ate," answered the Kid.

Dusty turned and studied his friend's face. When the Kid's voice took on that innocent note and he looked as saintly as a choirboy trying to win a good-conduct prize, he knew more than he admitted about the subject in question. Long experience had taught Dusty that questioning the Kid at such a time was a waste of time and so he did not bother.

"What about the rest of them?" Dusty asked, walking from the tepee and nodding toward the deserted campsite. "Where've they gone?"

"Back to their people, most likely," the Kid replied, glancing at his grandfather, who went to the tepee and looked inside. "When the women saw Fire Dancer dying the same way that folks who she cursed went under, they'd figure that her medicine had gone right back on her and pulled out afore it got them too."

"You came here, Cuchilo?" asked Long Walker.

"Yes, *tawk,*" admitted the Kid. "I found how she killed and laid a trap."

"It is well," the chief said, and let the tepee's door flap fall. "Sidewinder has not been here."

"He left no sign of it if he has," agreed the Kid. "Shall we wait to see if he comes?"

"No. After what has happened, I think the chiefs will listen and sign the treaty. Even the ones who waited to hear of Sidewinder will know that he has failed and be willing to make peace."

Mounting their horses the men rode away from the death camp. Dusty turned in his saddle and looked back at the tepee. He wondered what, if anything, the Kid knew about Fire Dancer's death. One thing was for sure, Fire Dancer's death was for the best; whether the poison had been administered accidentally or with deliberate intent. With her gone the white men who opposed the making of the treaty had lost a powerful and dangerous ally. Dusty doubted if Sidewinder would deal with white men on a friendly or cooperative basis without his mother forcing him to do so. A major threat to the chance of making a lasting peace lay dead in that tepee, and Dusty felt disinclined to inquire too closely into how she came to die.

Apart from the Kweharehnuh, who only the most optimistic observers had expected to come in, the majority of the Comanche people felt reconciled to making peace and living on a reservation. It seemed that only Sidewinder among the leaders might spoil the signing of the treaty and, with his band demoralized, scattered, or dead, he should prove less of a threat than he had only three days before. Dusty could not think how the chief might accomplish anything more.

On returning to the fort Dusty found that Temple Houston had not been wasting time in his absence. The lawyer obtained permission to visit Bristow, the captured whiskey peddler, and at first had no success with the man. So Houston made a plan and put it into operation. On the night that Dusty left, a shot through the window almost silenced Bristow—although, as Houston fired it, the man was in no great danger. Scared by what he regarded as a narrow escape, and believing that the people who had hired him aimed to take the easy way out of their difficulties regarding him, Bristow fell eagerly into Houston's suggestion that he save his neck by talking. While he knew little, Bristow told Houston the name of his contact and the only person he had met concerned with the plot. The peddler gave Houston a lead that subsequently brought about the arrest of several members of the ring involved in trying to disrupt the treaty council.

That evening a further piece of good news arrived. After some discussion the assembled chiefs of the Comanche decided to meet the white members of the treaty council with a view to making the final arrangements for signing the treaty.

Everything seemed all set for the successful conclusion of the council and the beginning of an era of peace between the majority of the Comanche nation and the people of Texas.

CHAPTER SIXTEEN

THE KID ACHIEVES A BOYHOOD AMBITION

The day of the treaty signing could not have been better. Overhead the sun shone brightly and only a light breeze stirred the air. General Handiman and the congressional committee sat at a table with all the papers before them, faced by the senior chief from each Comanche band that aimed to sign. To the right, formed up and wearing their best uniforms, sat three companies of cavalry and on the left of the table gathered a large number of Comanche men, women, and children all dressed to the height of fashion.

Every detail had been thrashed out in meetings, with the Kid standing by to act as interpreter for the Comanches, and at last the big moment had arrived. In a matter of seconds the treaty would be signed and a start at a lasting peace made.

Even as Handiman reached for the pen that lay ready for use, two shots rang out. Every eye turned in the direction of the shooter, looking out over the range and up a broken, bush-dotted slope. Six Indians, one of them sporting the warbonnet of a chief, sat their horses on the top of the slope.

"Sidewinder!" growled Long Walker as the warbonnet chief waved a Winchester carbine over his head.

"Hey, Comanches!" yelled Sidewinder. "What frightened dogs are you to let the white men force you to make peace? Who rides with me to live the old way?"

"Captain Connel, take men and—" Handiman began.

"Hold it, General!" interrupted the Kid. "That's not the way to handle it."

"Damn it, Kid," Handiman snorted. "We can't let him get away with it, even if I have to send all three companies after him."

"And how'd that look to the Comanche down here?" asked the Kid. "Sidewinder's likely only got those five jaspers with him. They're here to bust up the council, or die—and they won't die easy. Happen you send men against them in that broken stuff, they'll kill off plenty afore you get them. And while the fighting's going on it'll only take a wrong move on either side down here to spark off a shooting fuss."

All of which Handiman could see plainly enough when he paused for a moment. Sidewinder might have lost his medicine, but could easily regain it and pick up a following if the assembled *tehnap* and *tuivitsi* saw his small band inflicting heavy losses on the Army. And they stood a good chance of inflicting those losses, for the nature of the ground favored the Indians.

"What can we do?" Handiman growled, knowing that doing nothing would be as disastrous as sending forward soldiers.

For a moment the Kid did not reply, but his eyes went to the inkpots on the table. While one contained blue ink, the other held red ink of a thick kind to be used in making the Indians' marks.

"I reckon it's long gone time that me 'n' Sidewinder settled up old scores," the Kid said, and laid his rifle on the table.

Standing among the other honored guests at a distance behind the table, Dusty and Mark watched as the Kid peeled off his shirt. They exchanged glances and moved forward, for they guessed at what the Kid aimed to do and wanted to know if they might help in any way. While acting as interpreter for the Comanches the Kid wore his

Indian clothes and retained his armament. No Indian ever expected to have to lay down his arms at a peace council; that would be a sign he did not trust the other party involved.

Watched by the amazed white members of the crowd, the Kid stripped off his leggings and retained only moccasins, breechclout, and gun belt. A low mutter ran through the assembled Pehnane ranks, echoed by such of the other Comanches who knew the ways of the Quick Stingers, as the Kid poured red ink on to his palm and made the imprint of his hand on his chest. A quick grab raised his rifle from the table and he ran to where Manners stood holding the general's horse.

"Pukutsi!" roared the Kid, leapfrog-mounting over the horse's rump and snatching the reins from Manners's amazed hand.

"Pukutsi!" boomed back the voices of the Pehnane as they watched the Kid send the horse leaping forward in the direction of Sidewinder's party.

Sidewinder watched everything from where he sat his horse on the rim. While he had not seen the Kid since they were both boys, the chief knew that only one white man would act in such a manner. A snarl of fury left Sidewinder as he pointed at the charging Texan.

"Kill him!" he ordered.

Knowing that the only way to halt a man riding *pukutsi* in the Pehnane fashion was in the way their chief commanded, three of the braves sent their horses leaping forward to meet the Kid. Two of them carried rifles and the third held a bow to which he notched an arrow as his mount hit a full gallop.

Up swung the Kid's Winchester as he rode with the reins lashed up and hanging over the horse's neck, steering it with his knees. He sighted and fired, tumbling one of the rifle-armed braves from the saddle. Levering home another bullet the Kid changed his aim and saw the second brave lining a rifle at him. Flame licked from the

Kid's "yellow boy" as the brave fired at him. The Kid felt his mount jerk as the bullet struck it, heard its squeal, and sensed it collapsing under him. Before the horse's body crumpled and hit the ground, the Kid had left its saddle and landed on his feet with a catlike agility born in him and improved by long training. While landing he saw that his second shot had taken effect, for the other rifle-armed brave lay sprawled on the ground.

That left the third brave, and to the Kid's way of thinking the most dangerous. Armed with a bow and showing every sign of being a master in its use, the brave tore nearer. He ignored the fate of his companions, concentrating on the Kid with awesome intensity and determination to kill. Tense and ready the Kid saw the bow's string released and the arrow spring toward him. Timing his move perfectly he swung the Winchester and its barrel deflected the arrow's shaft. A quick swiveling movement swung the rifle back into line, slanting it up as the Kid prepared to leap aside and avoid being ridden down. He had no time to raise the rifle to his shoulder and fired from the hip. A flat-nosed .44 bullet drove in under the brave's jaw and burst out of the top of his head. Darting aside the Kid evaded the horse, and its lifeless rider crashed almost to his feet.

So busy had the Kid been in handling his first trio of attackers that he did not notice the remaining pair of Sidewinder's companions approaching. They came on foot, one carrying an Army Colt and the other wielding a war club. Firing on the run the Colt's user lacked the ability to aim accurately and missed. Before he could cock his revolver he paid the penalty. Still held hip high the Kid's rifle spat and its bullet tore into the Waw'ai's left breast and tumbled him backward.

The last brave charged in from the Kid's right side, so close that there would be no time to turn the rifle. Instead the Kid hurled his Winchester at the other's head. Throwing up his left arm the Waw'ai knocked the rifle aside and his other hand swung the war club at the Kid. The two-pound flint head—six inches long, with a width of three inches at one end and tapering to two inches at the other, secured by green rawhide, which shrunk and dried almost to the consistency of iron, to a sixteen-inch wooden shaft—whistled through the air. Swiftly the Kid twisted his body, bending it under the arc of the club's head. While doing so the Kid drew his bowie knife and swung a wicked backhand slash. Razor-sharp steel bit into the Waw'ai's belly, laying it wide open. A scream left his lips, the war club dropping from his fingers, and his hands clawed down at the terrible gash in his body. Staggering a few steps the Waw'ai sank to his knees and fell forward, writhing, on his face.

A bullet tore over the Kid's head and he flung himself forward in a rolling dive that carried him into cover. There had been no time to collect his rifle, and he drew the old Dragoon as he landed. Peering cautiously around the rock behind which he had landed, the Kid saw no sign of Sidewinder. Clearly the chief retained sufficient respect for his old enemy's shooting ability to take no chances.

Rising, the Kid darted from cover to cover up the slope. He went fast, but no shots came his way. Not for a moment did he think that Sidewinder had fled. While the chief might not relish a fight, he could not avoid one if he hoped to show his face among the Comanche again. Sidewinder and the last of his followers had come to the treaty council in a desperate bid to regain their lost medicine and so must be willing to die trying. Sidewinder knew that and had hidden somewhere, hoping for a chance to finish the Kid. If he did so, there might be braves willing to rally to him, enough to ruin the council.

Coming to a halt on the slope the Kid stood erect and looked around him.

"No Father!" he roared in Pehnane Comanche. "Come and fight, lame dog. This is no time to run as you did when we last met. Show yourself and I'll kill you as my father killed Bitter Root."

The vicious crack of the chief's carbine came after the Kid's words, every one of which had been spoken as a deadly insult. To call a name-warrior by the title he had held as a child was bad enough, but using the name of a dead father offered an even greater insult.

"He's been hit!" Mark Counter gasped, and a rumble of sound rose from the other members of the watching crowd as the Kid spun around, dropping revolver and knife, then crashing down to roll out of sight.

Thrusting himself from the bushes in which he had hidden, Sidewinder limped forward. A savage grin twisted the chief's face as he advanced to where he had last seen the Kid. In falling the Kid had gone into a gash torn in the slope at some time by a heavy flood of water, but since grown over. Sidewinder might have hesitated to follow so dangerous an enemy into that kind of area—even in their youth the Kid had few equals at the art of concealment, silent movement, and stalking—but the sight of weapons gave him heart. With his rifle lying back down the slope and the Colt and bowie knife in plain sight, the Kid had no weapons with which to defend himself.

Discarding his carbine for the better close-quarters handling qualities of the Army Colt he had taken from Salmon's body, Sidewinder advanced down the gash's side. He could see no sign of the Kid, yet felt sure that his bullet had taken effect. Possibly the other, badly wounded, had crawled into some cover and only needed finding to be finished off.

A hand came out from under a bush, took hold of Sidewinder's good ankle, and heaved at it. Sidewinder had never been a skilled player at *nanip'ka,* Guess over the Hill, where boys hid and the one from beyond the hill had to locate them. So he failed to see the Kid. With a yell he tumbled backward and his Colt fired a wild shot into the air. Like a flash the Kid lunged forward, meaning to land on the other's body and clamp hands on his throat. Poor *nanip'ka* player Sidewinder might be, but he could move fast. Constantly bearing the brunt of carrying him, his good leg had extra strength. Its foot rammed against the Kid's body, halted his progress, and hurled him aside. He landed rolling, and Sidewinder sat up, lining the Colt. As a bullet cut the air over his head, the Kid caught up a rock the size of a baseball and snapped it in Sidewinder's direction. His aim proved to be better than the chief's, for the rock caught Sidewinder in the face. However, the Kid knew he could not reach Sidewinder before the other recovered, and going closer made him a larger target. Instead he rose and flung himself up the slope. Blood trickled down Sidewinder's face but he did not let that interfere with his intention. It was kill or be killed now.

The Army Colt roared and the Kid felt lead slam into him, tearing through the fleshy part of his thigh. Exerting all his will he flung himself forward and his right hand reached out. He felt the cold, comforting touch of the Dragoon's walnut grips under his palm and closed his fingers around the butt. Already Sidewinder was coming up the slope, traveling fast despite his injured leg, determined to get in so close that he could not miss. Up came his Colt, lining toward the Kid.

Rolling over, the Kid brought up the Dragoon and held it cocked ready for use. An instant before Sidewinder felt sure of his aim, the Kid fired. Not for the first time the Kid found cause to be thankful for keeping that heavyweight, out-of-date handgun. The soft round lead ball struck with shocking force, hurling Sidewinder backward even though it only struck him in the shoulder. Before the chief recovered, or had a chance to, the Kid sat up, took careful aim, and sent a second bullet into the other's chest.

Rising, the Kid stood for a moment, then limped to where his knife lay. He took up the big weapon and approached Sidewinder. Bending down the Kid gripped the dead chief's hair and dragged his head up from the ground. Around came the knife, its blade ready to bite into flesh and remove the scalp. The fighting madness ebbed slowly away and his left hand loosed its grip of the hair. There at his feet lay his old enemy. Loud Voice and Comes for Food, the friends who had died saving the Kid's life, had been avenged at last. With Sidewinder dead the treaty could be signed. The old days had gone forever and the Kid could not take the scalp.

Slowly the Kid turned. Walking to where his Colt lay, dropped when he took up the knife to scalp his dead enemy, he picked it up and holstered it. Sheathing the bowie knife he limped up the slope and looked at the treaty council.

"Well," he mused as his friends ran up the slope toward him, "We've done it now. I sure hope that it's the right thing now it's done."